Puncturing the Deepest Curse

By

Mahogani Reign

Dynamic Image Publications presents
Puncturing the Deepest Curse
By Mahogani Reign

Edited by: Christian Cashelle

Manufactured in the United States of America

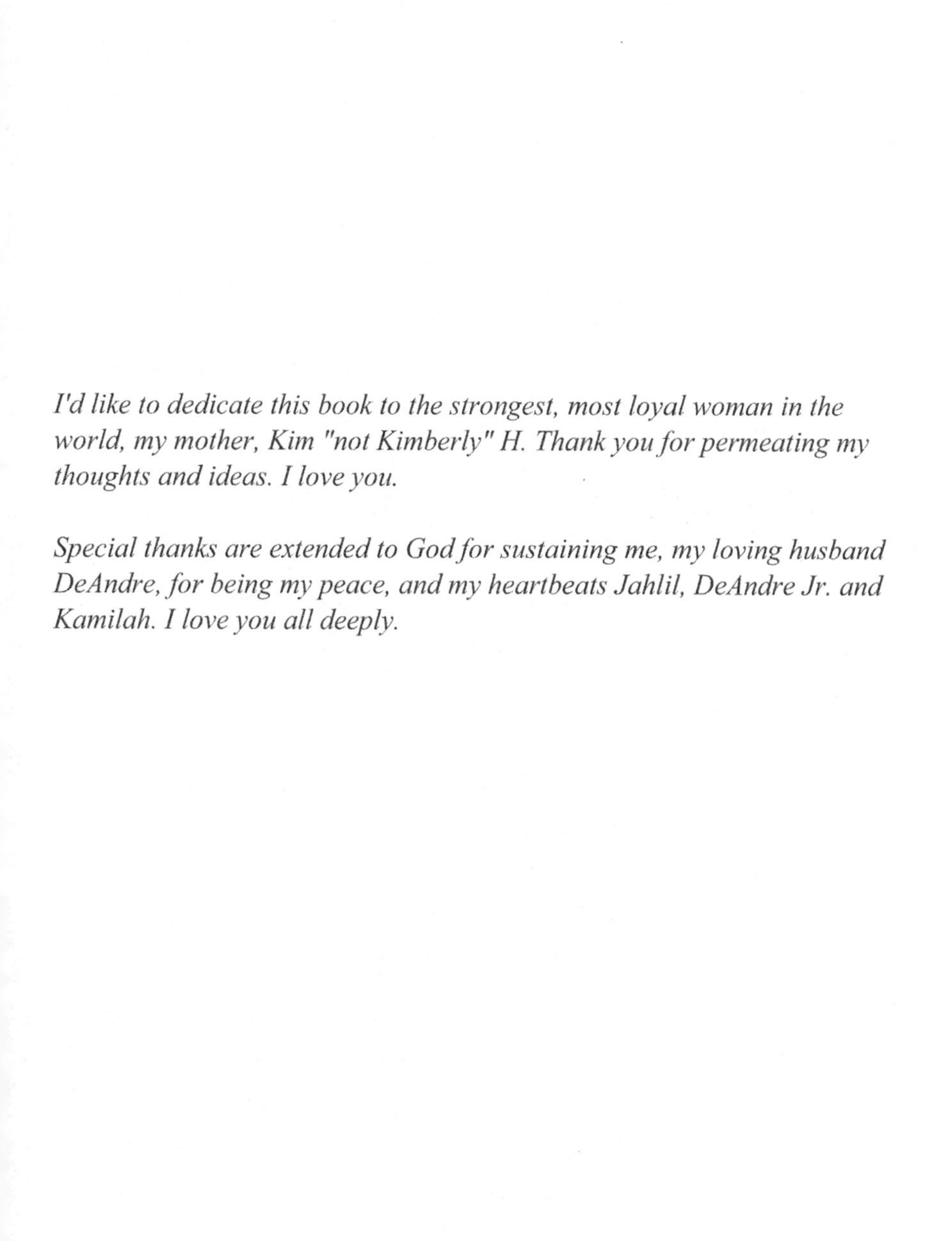

I'd like to dedicate this book to the strongest, most loyal woman in the world, my mother, Kim "not Kimberly" H. Thank you for permeating my thoughts and ideas. I love you.

Special thanks are extended to God for sustaining me, my loving husband DeAndre, for being my peace, and my heartbeats Jahlil, DeAndre Jr. and Kamilah. I love you all deeply.

When accidental tragedies happen, it's helpful to figure out what variables caused the accident in the first place. We all naturally seek comfort in knowing what could of have been done to prevent it. "Second nature" is to blame. We all want to brace ourselves before a tragedy. But what do you do when the tragedy lives in a person? Is the instinct of looking at the variables, pre cursors and circumstances still a priority?

Or is it easier to let that tragedy play out and move on?

There's no right or wrong answer. You see, Tragedy is a boastful, intentional, adolescent imprecation. It evolves to a curse if it's ignored and never dissected. It comes like a thief in the night, connects itself to families, and takes their last name. Its clever enough to lay dormant sometimes. Its strong enough to disguise itself as a blessing.

Love can overshadow Tragedy if you feed it. However, Love gets ignored just like Tragedy does sometimes. Where Love is absent Fear is present. And Fear.....Fear is the primary food for Tragedy.

Have you addressed the curses plaguing your family? Do you ignore them? Have you fed Love lately?

In this story, Tragedy grew up to be Curse and overstayed its welcome. It never left even after Love was fed. Love has to eat for generations to become strong enough just to battle Curse.

Love finally struck with enough power to puncture Curse. We'll just have to see if it was enough to kill it...

Chapter 1
Puncturing

"That's why darling it's incredible...that someone so unforgettable...thinks that I am...unforgettable, too."

As Jen sang a song about true love to her first born, she felt so dark inside. How did she get here?

Jen adjusted her Hijab. Although this headwrap had become apart of her identity, she knew it was merely a symptom of her trying to break the curse. The curse of brokenness, sickness, and pain that she was passing down to her daughter. Khadijah was a three-year-old princess. She was completely unaware of the storms raging in her own household.

As Khadijah sang the Nat King Cole tune with her mother, she danced around and smiled. She batted her beautiful big eyes, one of the better features she inherited from her mother. All of the sudden, they both heard the front door open and close. It was the man of the house coming home after a hard day of work. Jen's husband was the epitome of an ideal black man in 1992. Dr. Alex Mason, Clinical Psychologist was his full title. Alex was tall, dark, and handsome. He was charming and mysterious.

Khadijah ran towards the front door, "Daddy! Daddy!" she yelled, happily. He scooped her up in his arms.

"How's my great princess?"

"I'm singing to Mommy!" she beamed with pride.

As Jen walked into the room, she faked a smile, "Hey, honey. I put your dinner in the oven and Hasaan is asleep in his crib."

With Khadijah still in his arms, Alex walked close to Jen with a snarl.

"Thanks for dinner, but for your information, I don't care to know the whereabouts of that child. You don't even care that I just got off of work and yet you mock me?" He scolded.

Jen knew what would happen next.

She began to tremble and clench her teeth as anxiety crept through her body. Alex gently placed his daughter down and asked her to go into her brother's room to play. As Khadijah skipped away, Alex balled up his fist and punched Jen in her shoulder. Jen would usually try to fight back but after 4 years of this abuse she could not.

As she screamed from the physical pain and emotional blows, Khadijah heard it all. Sadly, since this had become a regular occurrence, she found her own way of coping. She envied the innocence of her baby brother because he had no idea what was going on. Khadijah would lock the door and hide under the bed when her dad turned into the devil.

The outburst her father had was because he didn't believe Hasaan was his child. He had no evidence that his wife was unfaithful. In fact, there was more evidence to the opposite. Jen was a beautiful woman. She had long, naturally wavy hair, a medium build with just enough curves and light caramel skin. Her teeth were white and her eyes were big, beautiful, and deep. To prove herself to her husband, Jen conformed to everything Alex wanted. She joined The Nation of Islam with him, wore a Hijab, and even cut off her family to be with him. He never allowed her to shop or have free time. Despite all, she was an amazing, doting wife and fantastic mother.

Alex hired a seamstress to come and dress her and the children with customized clothing. The house he bought them was payment enough in his eyes and Alex felt that Jen should be grateful to be home all day. Still, her beauty inside and out was too intimidating and he questioned her faithfulness. So with no logical reasoning, he requested a paternity test from his wife.

Later that night, Jen found a number she'd gotten from a loved one at the mosque. She gathered pictures, birth certificates, and warm clothing. Her plan was to leave when Alex left for work the next morning.

As hours passed and night approached, Jen was consumed with guilt. She looked around her beautiful subdivision home and thought about how she had been admired by so many women. Her own mother and sister fell jealous at the sight of the his and her sinks in her bathroom. Was she making the right choice?

Jen walked down the hallway and stopped to look at Khadijah and Hasaan sleeping. She thought about how she named them both with purpose and how damaging a life like this could unravel that purpose before it even began. She loved them with all of her heart and decided instead of embracing the curse like her family had with her, she would fight it with bloody fists and her last breath if she needed to.

The next morning after Alex left for work, in the cold of November, Jen packed her small grey Toyota like she was playing a serious game of Tetris. She left a little space in the back for Khadijah and a little space in the front for Hasaan's pumpkin seat.

"Mommy? Where are we going?" Khadijah asked innocently.

Jen wiped her eyes and in a Mr. Rogers fashion replied, "We are going to our new house!"

The drive was very sober and scary, but they arrived at the Hope and Refuge Battered Women's Shelter of Kansas City. As they pulled to the front, Khadijah was filled with excitement.

"Wow, Mommy this house is soooo big!"

With relief in her heart from escaping the abuse, Jen realized her and her children now lived in a shelter. She had no clue what was to come but she felt better knowing Alex would never hit her again.

However, the pain remained.

When Jen and her babies first walked into the facility, the cleanliness and white walls were reminiscent of a hospital. There were staff members walking around, identifiable by name tags. Jen held Hasaan on her left hip and held Khadijah with her right hand. She felt relief when a staff member approached her.

“Hello Jen?” she asked, carefully.

Jen smiled and responded soberly, “Yes, it’s me and this is Khadijah and Hasaan.” Khadijah was so excited she pulled and tugged at her mother’s hand.

The staff member crouched down until she was eye level with Khadijah and smiled warmly.

"Nice to meet you, Khadijah. We are so happy to have you and your family. We have a play area that I think you are going to love. Do you like doll houses?" she asked.

Khadijah jumped and swung her ponytails. "Yes, I loooove doll houses. I also like Elmo and Mr. Rogers. Can I watch Mr. Rogers, too?"

The lady chuckled and made eye contact with Jen. "Well, that's perfect because we love Mr. Rogers and Elmo, too!" She grabbed Hasaan's tiny hand and wooed him over with baby talk. He broke a smile and laughed. "By the way, my name is Linda. I'm one of the case managers at the facility. After I show you your room, I'll give you a tour and go over a little housekeeping."

Linda spoke very calm and precise. She was a white woman with fair skin and ash blonde hair. She wore very little makeup so her freckles showed. She had the most beautiful and mysterious deep set, grey eyes.

As she led them down a long hall, Khadijah saw other families in passing. She noticed there were no daddies in this new house. It's almost as if Linda heard her mind wandering when she began to tell them more about the facility.

"This safe space is only for women and children. We take great pride in keeping our location confidential. As you get to meet the other women, it is completely up to you about how much you want to disclose about yourself. We have a no pictures policy in place to respect confidentiality as well.

We serve three meals and three snacks daily. All of your toiletries and hygiene items are in your room, readily available, unless you have a preference and want to provide your own. There are many programs within our facility that are here to assist you and your transition to self-sufficiency and wellness," Linda explained.

"I came through this program after escaping a toxic situation myself. They helped me so much. With access to funding, I was able to go back to school and receive my degree and apply for a job here," Linda shared. Jen was surprised. Linda looked so young and privileged.

Jen was grateful for Linda's transparency and felt more at home. She figured if Linda didn't look like what she had been through then the same could be true for herself. She was very confident with her decision to leave. It was just hard to embrace the unknown. Where Jen was from, women didn't leave their husbands. If the man provided and kept coming home, the wife stayed and that was that.

Jen was sure some of her friends and even family would call her crazy for leaving her well off husband, regardless of the circumstances. It wasn't about them though.

She would die before she would willingly let Hasaan learn how to abuse and break down a woman.

She would die before she would willingly show Khadijah how to be a punching bag for a man.

Chapter 2
A Family is a Family

Time heals wounds like no other. Jen followed the plan at the women's shelter. They provided comfort where there was pain, family where there was loneliness, and hope for a better life. Khadijah received therapy appropriate for her age.

"Don't talk about it and chances are she will forget since she's so young," the counselors told Jen.

Over the course of a year, Jen was able to divorce Alex, prove Hasaan was his son through paternity testing (which was very embarrassing), move her little family to a small house, and even furnished it. She found a job at a salon in the mall as a stylist. Life was looking up.

Jen began to mend her relationship with her family after leaving Alex. Jen had an older sister named Kathy. Kathy was the opposite of Jen. Jen was quiet and dry humored. Kathy was bossy and traditional. Jen was lighter skinned and slimmer. Kathy was darker skinned and thicker. Jen was free spirited and fair. Kathy was strict and controlling.

Although the two of them were night and day, having family around was therapeutic for Jen. Jen's mother, Lola, had 4 children: Ray, Kathy, David, and Jen was the youngest. Their relationship was strange. They had a lot of family secrets, but hey, family is family right?

Kathy agreed to help Jen out with her children while she worked. At the time, Khadijah was 5 and Hasaan was 2. Khadijah was always so excited to go over Aunt Kathy's house. She was so stable and went out of her way to make her niece and nephew comfortable. After all, Jen was paying her. Aunt Kathy was also happy to see her son get a chance to spend more time with his cousins. Her son's name was Damon. He was a 15-year-old giant. Damon was 5'10" and beyond husky. Aunt Kathy could throw down in the kitchen and her son was the evidence. He was a great big cousin and was willing to help his mom anyway he could. However, as the only child, he also felt a little jealous when Khadijah and Hasaan would come over. They would get more attention than him.

One day when Khadijah and Hasaan came over, Aunt Kathy had to run to the store and asked Damon to watch the kids. He had no problem doing it. After Aunt Kathy left, Hasaan fell asleep.

Khadijah was a very playful and happy child. She loved hugs and was very smart for her age. She ran up to Damon and jumped on his back. He ran around, jumped, and made horsey noises! She was so happy to have such a fun, big cousin. Damon was sweet and nice and Khadijah started to forget about her father and his abuse. She felt she didn't need her father as long as she had Damon.

That was a lot of responsibility to put on a teenager, but all she knew was that he was as big as a man and he treated her like a big kid. He let Khadijah listen to the music with cursing. He shared his candy and chips. He even let her try pork. Her mom said Khadijah and her brother couldn't eat pork but it actually tasted good. She loved music and Damon had a collection she was obsessed with. Spending time with him was the highlight of Khadijah's life!

Damon was in charge while Aunt Kathy was gone. He made sure Hassaan was asleep and asked Khadijah to come to his room. She skipped, danced, and jumped on his bed. She loved to kick it with her big cousin. He turned on the boom box and pulled some of Khadijah's favorite candy out of his drawer. It was a sugary gel candy that you could squeeze out and lick. Her favorite flavor was blue.

"Dijah, do you want some Squeezy Candy?"

Khadijah jumped on the bed and yelled, "Yeeees!"

As she jumped, her barrettes clicked and clacked. Jen always kept Khadijah's hair so pretty. She had on a white tank top and gray long johns. Khadijah had no idea what she was saying yes to.

Damon pulled his pants down. He had the same private part as her baby brother. She saw it when her mommy gave her brother a bath or changed his diaper.

Damon squeezed the candy on his penis and told her the only way she could get the candy was to lick it off. Even though she felt it was weird, Khadijah did it anyway. She didn't like the candy anymore, so she stopped.

Damon covered her mouth and told her to be very quiet or he would have his dog attack her. Khadijah started crying.

He growled, "Shut up or I'll kill you!"

Damon pulled her pants down and hurt her very badly.

Khadijah was so hurt and scared as she ran to the bathroom. She wished her mommy was there. She peed in the toilet and when she wiped herself there was blood. Khadijah stayed in the bathroom for 15 minutes washing her private parts. She felt so sick and dirty. She was about to turn 6 and felt the burden of an adult woman.

Even though she was innocent in all of this, Khadijah felt bad for her cousin. Damon was in his room crying. She walked in and asked if he was okay. As a victim, Khadijah felt bad for making her cousin cry.

Damon said he was so sorry and begged Khadijah not to tell Aunt Kathy. She promised that she wouldn't say anything to anyone.

When Aunt Kathy came back home, Khadijah used her best acting skills to act like nothing happened. Aunt Kathy told the kids it was bath time. She wanted them to be ready for bed when Jen picked them up. Khadijah had school in the morning. She was in kindergarten. Aunt Kathy let Khadijah take her own bath and just monitored her since she was 5 years old. Khadijah washed up like she always did but purposely didn't wash her private parts. They still burned from what Damon did to her.

"Khadijah, wash that coota box girl!" Aunt Kathy yelled.

Khadijah wiped it softly with a towel.

Aggravated, Aunt Kathy took the towel from her, lathering it up with soap as she fussed. "You gotta soap the towel up or you'll be stinking. And scrub..."

Khadijah used all of the strength her little body could gather to not cry as her Aunt dragged a rough washcloth and burning soap across her gentle, bruised vagina.

Aunt Kathy continued to fuss.

"See, your mama teaching you that Muslim mess but ain't taught you to wash your cootie. Dry off so I can get Hasaan washed up and ready before your mama gets here!"

Khadijah dried off and felt dead inside. She wrapped herself in a towel and crept by Damon's room to her aunt's room. Khadijah looked around the room for the lotion and started to cry.

She prayed that she found the lotion and that Aunt Kathy didn't ask Damon to bring it. Sometimes, he would bring it and see Khadijah without clothes. It was never an issue before but at this moment she could pee on herself out of fear. Khadijah trembled so badly that her teeth clattered. She looked under the bed and was relieved to find the bottle of lotion. In that moment, she valued it more than anything she'd ever wanted. Khadijah put the lotion and her clothes on so fast that she got dizzy.

Aunt Kathy brought Hasaan in wrapped up in his towel. He was happy and so cute. Her baby brother was once again spared from the trauma. She envied him, but she would die for him. He was the only male that she knew who was good. In Khadijah's eyes, men were there to seem nice and fun but always ended up hurting you. Just like her daddy did to her mommy. Just like Damon did to her.

Jen arrived and got the kids settled into the car.

"Did you have a good time at Aunt Kathy's?"

Khadijah faked a smile and said, "Yes. I'm just really sleepy..."

Jen was so grateful for her sister's help. Daycares seemed so scary. She didn't want just anybody keeping her kid because anything could happen.

Thank Allah for family.

Chapter 3

The Choice

Khadijah gazed at her recorder tapes and her red boombox in shear delight. Her mom was the coolest mom in the world. She bought Khadijah a 6-piece set of recordable tapes so she could record all of her favorite songs on the radio. She loved TLC and would imagine she was Chilli, singing all of her parts and adlibs. Music was Khadijah's solace.

Khadijah was in 1st grade and so excited to learn about everything. She loved writing, reading, math, and especially music class. Her teachers adored her and her classmates all wanted to be her friend.

Jen was flourishing as a successful hairstylist and it showed in her children. She kept Khadijah and Hasaan dressed to the nines. Tommy Hilfiger, Nike, Nautica, and Ralph Lauren were always a part of their wardrobe. Hasaan kept a fresh haircut. Khadijah kept a fresh hairstyle and the latest jewelry. From the outside looking in, they were living it up.

The courts gave Alex a chance to have supervised visitation with Khadijah and Hasaan, but unfortunately he never showed up. After 3 missed visits, Jen was granted full custody. She felt like she was finally free from Alex and starting to get her groove back. Finally, after all of that hell, she could experience a taste of heaven.

Khadijah knew how happy her mom was becoming. That's why she couldn't tell her what had been happening to her for the past year.

Damon may have promised to not hurt her again, but he did. Over and over again. With each incident, he robbed Khadijah more and more of her innocence and taught her first hand about manipulation and lies. Instead of it being his shameful secret, Khadijah felt as if it was hers.

One day while she was at school, they called the entire 1st grade down for an assembly. There were nice people there to talk about abuse. They handed out pamphlets and talked about the different types of abuse. Mental abuse was when someone says things to you to make you feel bad. Physical abuse was when someone hits you. Sexual abuse was when someone touched you or hurt you on a private part of your body. They taught the children in a way that they could understand. The nice people also urged the students to let a trusted adult know if either ever happened to them.

Believe it or not, that was the first time Khadijah had a name for what Damon was doing to her. She really wanted to tell her mom now.

As Khadijah rode in the backseat of her mom's Toyota, she listened to the voices of TLC singing "Waterfalls." She thought about the assembly at school and trembled.

Khadijah took a deep breath. “Mama…”

"Yes, Khadijah?" Jen answered, perky and bright.

"...I don’t want to go to Aunt Kathy's house anymore."

Jen parked in front of her sister’s house and turned around to look at Khadijah. "Why don't you want to go?"

"...Because Damon is sexually abusing me,” Khadijah whimpered.

Jen didn't take her next breath. She felt as if her heart and stomach collided and began to crumble and spin. She gasped and asked Khadijah to repeat herself. She couldn't believe what her child said. Jen backed out of that parking spot and drove like a bat out of hell to her mom's.

Jen banged on the door and Lola answered.

"Jen I wasn't expecting you..."

With bloodshot eyes, Jen asked, "Mama, can you watch Khadijah and Hasaan for an hour?"

Khadijah was afraid. Her mom was very angry and acting strange. However, she was happy to spend time with her MeeMaw. Meemaw made the best grilled cheese sandwiches. Khadijah was also happy to be away from Damon.

After about an hour went by, Meemaw got a phone call that made her cry loudly. She told Khadijah and Hasaan they were spending the night. This hurt Khadijah because she thought her mom was mad at her. She wished so badly that she had her tapes so she could listen to Mariah Carey and TLC. They made her feel so special.

What she didn't know was that her mom wasn't mad at her. Jen was mad for her. She drove to Damon's high school and attempted to run him over with her car. The attempt failed and she was arrested and placed on a psych hold for 24 hours.

When Jen was released, she decided to press charges against her nephew for molesting her child. Jen picked Khadijah up with puffy eyes and no makeup. As she was about to leave, her mom asked her, "Jen, why put our family business out there that way? We could've handled this."

"Mama, are you serious?" Jen snapped. "I have a choice to make and whatever I do will affect Khadijah, just as it did me. I'm choosing my child. I refuse to keep this curse going! I won't brush this under the rug!"

She stormed out of her mother's house, determined to get justice for Khadijah.

Jen took her to the hospital where they gave her a vaginal exam. They confirmed Khadijah's hymen was broken and she'd been penetrated. Khadijah was numb through it all.

As they poked, prodded and questioned her, she wondered if she made the best choice by telling her mom.

Even in her pain, Jen knew she did. She would not allow her baby girl to be a victim of "brush it under the rug" abuse.

Charges were pressed, justice was served.

Khadijah was offered the best therapy and help available. She was free from Damon and the abuse. However, she still felt guilty. She couldn't see any family because they were all embarrassed and upset. Even her own grandmother was distant because she didn't agree with how the situation was handled.

The curse of the broken family was back and stronger than before. Khadijah felt like it was all her fault.

Chapter 4
The Three

"Look mom! Loooook!" squealed an excited 6-year-old Khadijah.

She was so proud of her sketches. Jen taught Khadijah how to write her name like a graffiti artist with bubble letters. She was definitely artistically inclined. All of the pain Khadijah endured was muted by her love for art and music. Music was her getaway and solace. She didn't care if it was Rock, Oldies, Hip Hop, or R&B.

"What do you think, Mom?" she asked Jen while batting her eyelashes over her pretty almond eyes.

Jen beamed. "I love it! You could be a famous artist!"

Khadijah held up another piece of paper and shook it around excitedly. "And Hasaan wrote the letter H! I taught him how, Mommy!"

"You're such a great big sister. I wish I had a sister like you!"

It was so important for Jen to make Khadijah feel good and happy about herself. It had only been two weeks since Khadijah's world was turned upside down. Jen felt so guilty.

Khadijah was prescribed antibiotics as a precaution in case she contracted anything from being raped by Damon. Jen thanked God that she hadn't. The courts also recommended that Khadijah see an at-home therapist for three weeks to give her strong coping skills to help with the trauma. Therapy gave Khadijah a reroute from trauma to triumph. Khadijah was actually relieved to be free from such a sick cycle. It was liberating.

Khadijah rocked back and forth while sitting on the floor. "Don't Speak" by No Doubt blared from the boombox. She sang along and continued to sketch with her little brother. Hasaan was such a sweet little boy. Khadijah loved her brother with all of her heart. Together they drew their names, flowers, and all sorts of shapes until Jen interrupted their fun.

"Hey, you guys come get ready for dinner. Go wash your hands!"

Khadijah took her painting to their bedroom. As she flipped the light switch, it didn't turn on. She flipped it three more times and realized the bulb went out. She walked into the dark room to sit the drawing on the dresser. At that moment, a surge of fear shot through Khadijah's body. She began to swallow but her throat was tightening up. Her breathing became shallow. She felt scared, guilty, and nervous. Her hands started to shake.

Jen appeared in the doorway and startled Khadijah.

"I need to replace this bulb. Are you okay, Khadijah?"

Khadijah lied, "Yes ma'am, I'm about to go wash my hands."

Khadijah felt as if she had already done enough to her family. She would hear her mom relive what happened to them over the phone. She heard her mom cry many nights. The last thing she wanted was to be a burden in another way. Khadijah washed her hands and sat down for dinner.

Jen was a very conscious black woman. She was raised on soul food. Everything was packed with butter, sugar, and pig parts. When she was a part of the Nation of Islam, she learned to cook healthier. That night she made baked barbecue drumsticks, cheddar spinach rice with eggs, wheat rolls, and orange sherbet for dessert. It smelled like love and favor in that apartment.

Jen talked to her children and allowed them to express themselves freely. When she came up, children were to be seen and not heard. Khadijah talked about how much she loved math and music. She also flexed her impressive spelling skills. Hasaan was only 3 years old so he chimed in when he got excited. His happiness mattered in this space, too.

As Jen spoke, Khadijah would hold on to every word. Jen's voice was so sweet and assuring. Her skin was the color of butterscotch and even though her beauty was captivating, so was her intellect. Khadijah would imitate her mom frequently.

She wanted to be her mom.

After the three of them finished dinner, Jen summoned Khadijah to take her medicine. The pink flavored amoxicillin liquid was a reminder to Jen that someone had hurt her baby. She prayed for her daughter daily and blamed herself for leaving Khadijah in that environment all those days. How could she not see the signs? She felt so disgusted and guilty.

Beating herself up was definitely not the answer. Jen knew, deep inside of her heart that she had to focus on herself, Khadijah, and Hasaan from here on out. As long as they had each other, everything would work itself out.

Khadijah skipped in excitement to take the medicine. It tasted so good, she was happy to take it. It became the highlight of her day. She took it in delight and went to bed.

The next morning, Khadijah walked into her school and saw her friend, Meghan. Meghan and Khadijah were thick as thieves. They told each other everything. Khadijah never told Meghan about what Damon did to her though. Favorite colors, songs, cheers, and toys were all fair game.

Meghan smiled and ran to give Khadijah a hug.

"I love your hair, Khadijah. You look like Brandy!" Meghan said before she began to sing. "Don't know what I'd ever do without you from the beginning to the end..."

Khadijah joined in singing and sang her best run to close it off.

"You don't have to show out," Meghan nagged.

"I wasn't showing out, I just love that song. I love Brandy." Khadijah said, defensively as she swung her fresh pinch braids. It took 13 hours at the African Braiding Shop to get them done.

"Well, look what my mom got me! Three new Lisa Frank folders!" Meghan said, proudly.

Khadijah wanted Meghan to feel special so she didn't mention that her mother had already bought her those same folders. "Wow! Those are so pretty! I wish I had them."

Khadijah hid those folders from Meghan until the last quarter of the school year.

Jen was advised by the social workers handling Khadijah's case that she should tell her teacher and principal about what happened. It was important for them to monitor her behavior. They were worried she would recluse or re-offend.

However, Khadijah wowed her teacher everyday. She walked in with the biggest smile and most positive attitude. She had been out of control inside for such a long time. She was determined to be the best student and friend.

There were some teachers that were intimidated by little Khadijah. Her name alone was so different in 1995. Khadijah spoke such proper English for a black child and some mistook her young professionalism for being disrespectful and too grown.

They just didn't know what she was battling.

Jen told Khadijah it would be her last year at Deemlin Elementary School. Khadijah was determined to leave behind a great reputation, one that showed no signs of the trauma she had endured.

Business was kicking for Jen and she was ready to move her babies to a nicer district. Khadijah was excited to get a fresh start and make new friends. She would really miss Meghan, but she was ready for friends that she didn't have to make feel comfortable.

She wanted friends who were on her level. Friends she could share her talents with. Only if they liked her talents, because she wanted to be liked. And pretty, she really wanted to be pretty like her mom. Not too pretty, though, because then a man might look at her and abuse her.

She didn't want to lose any more family.

That's why she had to make more friends so she can replace all of the family that was gone.

That would keep her mommy happy.

Little did Khadijah know she started a terrible habit when it came to friendships. This is when people pleasing and anxiety entered Khadijah's life. They worked daily to penetrate Khadijah's existence. They entered her mind first thing in the morning and swarmed her before she closed her eyes at night. She had to perfect everything and be the best, or else.

Everyone saw a strong little black girl on the outside and had no idea what storm was forming on the inside.

Chapter 5
Growing Pains

The next year of Khadijah's life went by so fast, it was more of a flashback than an actual memory. Her mom fell in love with a Navy soldier named Shaun. He was business minded just like Jen. He was strict, yet fair and a good provider. He helped Jen open her own salon. He took her on fancy trips, bought her a fresh white SUV, and had no problem helping spoil Hasaan and Khadijah.

Third grade was everything for Khadijah. At her new school she made new friends and got a reputation of being smart and fly. She was also introduced to orchestra. The orchestra instructor taught all of the 3rd graders together, but also pushed the ones who showed proficiency. Towards the end of the school year, they had a big performance to showcase all that the students had learned so far. Khadijah managed to be the most advanced violinist that year. The plan for the concert was that as the songs got more advanced, less students would play. Since Khadijah was the most proficient, she got her own song. She practiced tirelessly.

When the orchestra concert finally came, terror wasn't the proper word for how she felt. Her anxiety overwhelmed her, but it also fueled her to be amazing.

After she finished her song, Khadijah received a standing ovation from all of the proud parents. She looked into the audience to see her family and the only people there were Jen and Hasaan. She was grateful for them but couldn't help but notice her friend, Tasha, had two whole rows of family there to support her. Tasha only made it to the third song and had so many cousins and family there. Khadijah was confused. She felt that she wasn't good enough. She used orchestra and the spelling bee to overachieve. It meant alot to her to make others proud. This warped thinking spiraled into the 4th, 5th, and 6th grade.

Khadijah was a 12-year-old young woman by this point. Everything she did was articulately motivated. She hid people pleasing well. Her friendships were never honest due to her changing herself to please her friends. Khadijah did manage to find three real best friends. Ashley taught her the importance to valuing each other. She had a brain tumor and was dying from cancer. A child watching another child die is a sick and sad event. Khadijah, along with the help from her second best friend, wrote their very first song to encourage Ashley. Jaquelin, or Jackie as she called her, name the song, "Angel Girl." Engaging in creativity lit a fire in Khadijah like no other. Khadijah and Jackie had a bond that was unbreakable. Jackie was the type of friend that didn't play games. She was street smart, loyal and strong. She had the warmest smile, long hair, and stood at 4'10". Jackie frequently called Khadijah out on her people pleasing.

"Khadijah, don't be someone else in order to fit in!"

She only listened sometimes. The final bff was Kanesha. Kanesha wasn't as wise as Ashley or as loyal as Jackie, but she had issues like Khadijah.

Even though Kanesha would make Khadijah the butt of jokes, ignore her, and belittle her, she was Khadijah's favorite. They had so much in common. They were both smart, brown skinned, tall, creative, and into boys.

Jackie had such a stable home. Her parents were so involved. They wouldn't let her go some of the places Khadijah and Kanesha could. Most of the time Khadijah got to spend with Jackie was when she spent the night and went to church with Jackie and her family. Jackie's parents were the first healthy black marriage that Khadijah saw up close and personal. Jackie's mom was a virtuous woman. She was poised, professional, nurturing, loving, and beautiful. Her father was a real life hero. He was an educator, a coach, a preacher, and a doting father. Whenever Khadijah came over, he treated her as if she was his own. He was a glimmer of hope in her eyes. Where most men had been deviant, abusive, and careless; he was not.

After writing their first song together, Khadijah and Jackie realized they were musically gifted. They began to write many more songs, convinced that would be their meal ticket to stardom. One Saturday night when Khadijah was over, her and Jackie decided to remix hymns from the back of an old choir book. "Behold, Behold! I stand at the door and knock. If anyone hears my voice, I will open and come in." They made this old hymn sound like the next Babyface hit.

These girls sang as if they had been here before.

They sang together until Jackie's mom told them to get ready for bed so they wouldn't be tired for church in the morning. Jackie's household was so normal. Although Khadijah's mom tried to give her the world, there were still empty spaces. The family that was absent, the holidays her mom didn't care to celebrate, and the absence of a solid faith were all concepts that Khadijah wished she had. In the meantime, Khadijah would soak it all in while having sleepovers with Jackie.

As they fell asleep, Khadijah could smell the starch and heat from clothes being ironed and pink oil moisturizer in tied up heads. It was a pure comfort for her.

The next morning, Khadijah was so excited to get to church. Besides the awkward questions like, "Who's your mom? What church home do you belong to? Did you bring a shrug for those legs being out?" She loved everything about church. As she learned more and more about God, Khadijah noticed she had less and less anxiety. When the choir sang it felt like she was levitating. Khadijah was so in tune with the lyrics, harmonies, and chords, even at the tender age of 12, she cried during the sermonic selections. She was so grateful for all that God had brought her through.

Khadijah was dropped off at home on Sunday evening. She couldn't wait to call Kanesha and get on the phone with boys. All that holiness was lovely, but Khadijah loved the attention she got from boys. She loved to read her poetry and sing her songs on the phone. It was her version of the early Youtubers. Kanesha was on the same page. They would get on a three-way call with boys, flirt, and plan meetups to the movies.

When Khadijah walked in her front door, her mom was very frustrated and angry. She was cursing very loudly and Shaun was upset as well. Their relationship was in its 4th year and they were usually very private about their disagreements.

"Hey Khadijah," Jen snarled. "I hope you prayed for Mommy at church."

Assuming her mom was using rhetoric, Khadijah avoided eye contact. She saw Shaun carrying boxes to his truck. He didn't speak or say hi to her.

Jen had bloodshot, puffy eyes as if she had been crying all day.

"Don't look at that motherfucker. Cheating bastard! Get all your shit and get out my house. I don't ever want to see you again!" she yelled.

Even though Khadijah couldn't stand how strict Shaun was, he was a father figure and he helped her mom stay happy. All of the trips, bonding, and signs of normalcy were walking away. He seemed as if he was relieved.

"*Were we that bad?*" Khadijah wondered.

The limbo was coming again. The unknown fate.

Jen was so tired of life screwing her over. She needed an escape badly.

Chapter 6
The Great Fall

"Knock! Knock!"

Khadijah had been knocking for 2 minutes outside of her mom's door. Lately, Jen had been locking it. Her mom had a right to sulk. She was still sad about Shaun and their break up. People are allowed to be sad.

"Mom! Did you buy me more deodorant?"

Jen swung the door open with her head down. "I'm sorry, Khadijah. I'll have some for you when you get home, just use powder for now."

Jen went from one closed door to another as she dragged her feet to the bathroom.

Khadijah powdered her underarms so she wouldn't be musty. She already felt self-conscious because she was on her cycle. At 13, she was very aware of her body. She had been since she got her period at 9 years old.

As she and Hasaan prepared to leave for the bus stop, Khadijah noticed how unclean their town home had gotten. It had been 2 months since her mom and Shaun broke up. As a man in the military, Shaun naturally did most of the cleaning. Khadijah told herself that when she got home, she'd surprise her mom and make her happy by cleaning up.

The bus ride to school was mellow. There was a lot of fog since Spring was transitioning into Summer. Middle School was a trip. Khadijah had managed to get through almost all of 7th grade in one piece. Outside of the competition amongst the girls, unwanted and wanted attention from boys, boatloads of homework, and the pressure to always be cool, Khadijah was a natural. She never really belonged to a group or clique. She really vibed well with everyone.

After her last class, she couldn't wait to find Jackie so they could talk about fresh gossip from lunch. They sat together, laughed, and joked. They reminisced on a time earlier that school year when Jackie's dad, who they affectionately called "Pops," took them to the Juvenile Detention Center after finding them smoking Black & Milds in an alley. He staged a scare session where the entire center made it appear they would stay locked up the whole night. It wasn't funny at the time, but they laughed about it later.

It was amazing to Khadijah to have someone like Pops in her life. It surprised her how he went through the trouble of teaching her a lesson just to ensure she would get her act together. She honestly yearned for more structure. Lately her mother slacked in the parenting department.

As the bus pulled up to let Khadijah off, she noticed someone else had gotten evicted. The townhome complex would hire movers to empty out the units of the tenants who weren't current on their rent.

"*They should've paid their rent,*" Khadijah thought.

At that moment, her world stopped.

As she walked towards her home, Khadijah realized it was her personal items sprawled across the entrance lawn. Her keyboard, her bed, her clothes, all of their living room furniture...all there. Embarrassed, Khadijah ran home. As she walked into the house, she found her mother on the floor crying. The most beautiful woman in the world, her only support system, sat there helplessly. Her eyes were bloodshot red and her mouth was full of saliva.

"I'm so sorry, Khadijah," Jen sobbed. "We're being evicted. I'm gonna fix this, I promise."

Khadijah hugged her mom. "It's okay, Mama. Don't cry. I'm not mad."

Khadijah was a very mature and understanding teen. She empathized with her mother.

When Hasaan arrived, he cried and was extremely embarrassed. That didn't help the situation at all but it was a natural reaction for a child who had lost their home.

Pops showed up with a pickup truck and did his best to transport some of their items to storage so they wouldn't be stolen. The rest was a lost cause. He was truly family for such a thoughtful gesture.

Khadijah was embarrassed and disappointed, but to please her mom she didn't show it.

"*Where are we sleeping tonight if we don't have a home*?" she wondered.

However, Khadijah didn't ask. She just got in the car and rode. The car ride was long. The nice neighborhoods they were accustomed to faded away. As they approached what Khadijah knew as the hood, she began to bite her hangnails. This day had truly turned into a nightmare that she never saw coming.

They ended up staying with one of Jen's male friends. He only had a one bedroom apartment, but set up two futons in the living room. Jen and Hasaan shared one and Khadijah had the other to herself. Neither one of them slept well that night. Khadijah was so worried what all the other kids at school would say once word got around that her and her family were evicted. Khadijah's mind was racing.

"*First Shaun left, then her mom sold her salon, and now this? Was her mom so sad she couldn't handle business anymore? What happened?*"

She had so many questions. She was so afraid. Anxiety ate away at her.

After Khadijah finally dozed off, Jen tiptoed into her friend, Henry's room.

Behind the closed door, the two of them snorted and smoked crack cocaine. Jen hadn't used drugs since before she married her ex-husband, Alex. Her recent struggles took her over the edge. The reality that her new struggles were hers and hers alone made it even worse. She'd been hiding the habit from her children for months.

Her junk was starting to show.

Jen still dressed up and wore makeup daily. Outside of her recent weight loss and crumbling life, they had no reason to suspect their mother was on crack. Henry was an old friend of

Jen’s and even though he was addicted as well, he didn't want her on the streets. She stayed in the house and hid herself from the world and he supplied her habit. Henry enabling her habit made it hard for those around her to suspect what she was going through. After all, according to TV, crack heads had ashy mouths and stood on corners.

Filled with guilt, Jen got back into the bed with Hasaan and cried. The high was already gone. Her rock bottom was straight ahead. Jen didn't want her kids to know her secret. The weight of all her trauma was too heavy to carry anymore, so it fell.

Chapter 7

Plastic Spoons

The hood wasn't exactly what Khadijah expected. However, there's some truth in stereotypes. Where she was used to open spaces, friendliness, and endless outcomes, the hood was different. Homes and apartments were piled on top of each other. Friendliness was replaced by like-mindedness. Everybody thought the same. They had the same experiences, the same recollections, and the disadvantages were more like second nature.

Khadijah spent most of her summer escaping the hood. She would spend the night over anyone's house just to feel normal again. While Hasaan was always invited to go on road trips with Jen's best friend, Khadijah had to figure it out on her own. She guessed that Hasaan fit in better with them.

So she bounced from Jackie's home, to Kanesha's home, to random friends' homes that had lenient parents for weekend getaways. Most of their parents knew Khadijah was a good girl going through an unfortunate circumstance. What they didn't know was Khadijah was turning into a manipulating rebel.

Khadijah once convinced Jackie to have her over for the weekend just so she could spend time with boys in the neighborhood. She met up with a boy she had been talking to on the phone with named Rico. He was Puerto Rican and loved to talk about sex with Khadijah. She played along and told him what she would do to him if they ever had the chance. He was 16 so when they met up, he was ready to turn their conversations into a reality.

Rico met Khadijah at a mutual friend's house when their parents would be away at work. He led her to the bedroom, closed and locked the door. He had no intentions to satisfy her with foreplay. He was ready for her to back up what she bragged about. She took off her clothes, but she was afraid. She knew there were friends waiting on the other side of the closed door who also expected her to follow through on her words.

Khadijah laid down and watched carefully as he rolled a yellow condom down his erect penis. Without any warning he penetrated her and humped all of three minutes. It was terrible. She wasn't turned on so she was barely moist outside of the lubricant that was on the condom. Khadijah was also shocked by the penetration. When she masturbated before, she never inserted her fingers. She thought sex was just rubbing on the outside.

After Rico finished, he got up and put on his pants. He could tell Khadijah was a virgin by the way she was reacting and by how tight she was. He leaned in for a kiss to try to make atonement. She fought back tears and got dressed. She figured she would report to her friends that she was a master in the bedroom instead of being honest about how stupid she felt.

Rico began to ignore Khadijah's calls after that.

She realized she wasn't as ready for sex as she thought, but her eagerness to be wild was still strong. Lying to her mother and her friends' mothers got so easy because she was known for being a good girl. Khadijah manipulated all of them.

That summer, Khadijah not only lost her virginity, but she got drunk and smoked her first blunt. She was only 13.

She began to drift away from Jackie because her parents were too strict and wouldn't let Khadijah run the streets.

Kanesha's house was the best option.

Her mom was older and worked a lot so her place was ideal for sleepovers. Kanesha was just as fast as Khadijah was. They were two peas in a pod. Kanesha was tall, toffee brown skinned with long dark hair. She was mixed with something and it kept her in high demand. She was smart as a whip so she taught herself to speak Spanish. She became fluent because her brother married a Spanish speaking woman.

Khadijah inherited her mother's gift of beauty skills. She would make sure her and Kanesha had their hair, brows, and nails looking the best. They made a game of finding older guys in pairs so they could hang out with them. They'd talk to them on the phone on a 3-way call.

Khadijah had grown up really fast. She was tall, milk chocolate brown, fully developed and pretty as a picture. Her almond eyes, white teeth, and her way with words always lured in the boys she had eyes for. The two of them were jailbait.

They even began to have interest in porn. Neither one of them was truly interested in sex though. They more so loved the attention it brought and the feeling of being aroused. Khadijah learned her lesson with Rico.

As the summer ended, Khadijah couldn't escape the hood any longer. She had to face the shift in her life. Jen had no idea Babylon had set up inside of her daughter. She was too fried.

She did manage to get Khadijah and Hasaan registered for school and buy them clothes and shoes. Even amongst all the adversity, Jen wanted to be a mom. She felt bad enough her kid's lives had been uprooted. She didn't want to send them to school looking raggedy.

Khadijah was so nervous. Going to school in the hood gave her so much anxiety. Music, writing, and masterbation made for a temporary fix. She didn't know she felt the need to masturbate under stress until she found herself doing it so often. The orgasms were addicting and they calmed her mind. She was so embarrassed by it though. It made her feel dirty and alone.

However, it remained her secret coping mechanism.

The move to the city resulted in Khadijah having more responsibility. She had to step up her big sister duties. She was given a ride to school and since her school let out before her little brother's, she would walk to get him and then together they would walk home.

Of course, Khadijah stuck out like a sore thumb when she started school. All of the other 8th graders were familiar with each other. It was strange to switch schools the final year of junior high. She was pretty, so she got along with the boys immediately. The girls weren't mean, but they wondered why she talked so white. Khadijah eventually made friends and kept pushing.

Khadijah was only partially honest with her new friends. Even though she was managing her new social life at school, her home life was in shambles. Jen taught Khadijah how to handwash clothes because they no longer had a washer and dryer. She would clean her and Hasaan's clothes and make whatever was around for dinner.

Some nights Jen would be there and some nights she wouldn't. Nothing was warm or loving about that apartment. The walls were off white and had chipped paint. There was no privacy since it was a one bedroom. It was a claustrophobic nightmare. It smelled like old smoke and moth balls. With the entrance only two feet from her futon, Khadijah felt like she might as well be in a jail cell. Dreaming of better days and listening to music helped, but the frustration, confusion, fear, and sadness she felt was powerful.

Hasaan's laugh meant a lot to her during that time. He was still so young and innocent. Khadijah's will to try to and be happy, even under such unfit living conditions, had to prevail.

Since Henry normally lived alone, he only had 5 spoons. Him and Jen were chasing drugs, so they didn't think to buy dishwashing liquid. Even though Khadijah was living a lower quality of life, she was still a princess at heart. She started bringing home plastic spoons from school so her and her brother could eat from clean utensils.

Sometimes, just to break away from the sadness and depression that the apartment brought, Khadijah would get lost in her music. Whenever she sang along to Mariah Carey she would add her own ad libs and make believe that she was a featured artist on the song. She imagined that instead of smelling mothballs and smoke that she smelled expensive scented candles and new furniture.

When Khadijah was home alone, she would take her music to the bathroom with her. She would mix soap and water together and use it to clean the mirror until it was spot and streak free. Somehow looking into a clean mirror gave her the illusion that she wasn't poor anymore.

Khadijah loved to sing in front of the mirror and act out the lyrics to what she was singing. She would even cry while performing to the mirror if the song brought out enough emotion. Her tears weren't from sadness in those instances. Khadijah truly was performing. She felt like she had to keep up with her superstar qualities for when all of the suffering was over. Just in case a talent agent found her or she ever got a chance to audition for anything, she would be ready.

Khadijah didn't have it in her to be 100% practical. Being practical meant she accepted her environment and living conditions. Being practical meant she was a dirty, black teenager with nothing. These mini concerts she threw for herself kept her hopeful, far away from practicalness. With hope at the forefront, Khadijah was an undiscovered star in between blessings.

When Fall began to turn into winter, Khadijah felt a renewed optimism. She hoped the season change brought along change in her life.

One day, Jen was home after school and told Khadijah and Hasaan all they had was sardines for dinner. Hasaan ate it and thought it was cool. Khadijah went hungry that night.

Jen felt so low. She wanted to get clean and had no idea where to turn or start. She looked at Khadijah and Hasaan sleeping and promised herself she'd get better. She woke Khadijah up and sat on the edge of the futon. Confused, Khadijah sat up on the futon sleepy eyes.

"Khadijah, I have to tell you something..."

"What's wrong, Mama?" Khadijah asked.

Jen began to sob. Khadijah noticed how frail her mother's body had gotten. She also smelled a sweet stench coming from her pores and her complexion was dull.

"I need help. I'm using drugs and it's making me sick. I'm going to have to leave you and Hasaan for a while so I can get better." Jen was jittery and twitchy.

Khadijah protested, "No, Mama! I can help you. You don't have to leave. I love you. Everything is going to be fine. I can help with Hasaan even more. I won't ask you to buy me anything either. We have to stay together, okay?"

Khadijah's eyes were optimistic and nurturing.

Realizing her daughter didn't understand what was just revealed to her, Jen hugged Khadijah tight. She cried into her daughter's shoulder. Khadijah rubbed her mother's frail back and tasted her own salty tears as they fell down her face.

The next morning, Jen moved her children out of Henry's apartment. As they rode in a black Cavalier packed to the brim, Khadijah realized they were driving towards the county. She was excited to be close to her stomping grounds, but they pulled up to an unknown building with people lined up outside the door.

It was a homeless shelter.

Jen turned around and assured her children it would just be a few nights. Khadijah was grateful. They were assigned cots in a room. Khadijah guarded her walkman player and journal. Although the shelter wasn't familiar, she felt safe and warm and the food was good. They served complete meals with a meat, two sides and a piece of bread.

The other families were polite. They all had a familiar look of shame on their faces. The shelter had yellow and green walls which was more personal and inviting than her last home. Home began to be such a jaded term for Khadijah. She didn't understand the assurance behind that word anymore.

Khadijah noticed there were other teens in this shelter. They didn't have a mom. They were on their own. One was a girl and the other she couldn't tell if they were a boy or a girl. She saw them in passing going to the restroom or leaving the cafeteria. Khadijah wanted the courage to approach them and make friends but she felt as if she didn't have much to offer. She was embarrassed by her life. She opted for writing in her composition book instead.

Khadijah journaled her feelings, goals, and dreams during any spare time that she had. She also had a lot of time to ponder on what her mother shared with her the other night. She wondered how many other people in the shelter were on drugs.

After two nights at the shelter, Khadijah overheard her mom on the phone thanking someone.

After that call, Jen packed her children up again and drove a short distance. They pulled up to a familiar house. It was the Aunt Janice's house. Aunt Janice had extra room in her basement and extended her home to Jen and her children. Aunt Janice was Khadijah's paternal aunt. Khadijah had no relationship with her father, but Aunt Janice stayed connected through the years. She was so happy to be around family.

She was eclectic, smart, loving, and warm. She had 5 children; three were adults and the twins were a year younger than Khadijah. Aunt Janice had house rules and she went to church on Sundays. She was a normal, healthy mother. Jen loved the normalcy that the new living arrangement brought to her children. However, she still wanted to chase her high. Aunt Janice wouldn't allow it.

After one week, they packed up again. This time they drove towards the city. Khadijah cried in private because she didn't want to leave Aunt Janice's house. They had lived in 3 different places within the course of one month. This type of living was so dysfunctional. Khadijah braced herself for their next home.

As they pulled up, Jen looked at Khadijah. "This is my sister's house. You all will be staying with her for a while. I know you might be worried because of Damon, but that was a long time ago so you'll be okay..."

Silence filled the car. Time stood still. Apparently Aunt Kathy moved from the house Khadijah knew. This house was different. It was scarier because of who she feared was inside of it.

Khadijah was terrified. Her heart began to race and skip. She hadn't seen Aunt Kathy or Damon in 8 years. Not since Damon was charged with raping her. She began to tremble. She had a lump in her throat that wouldn't go away. She had on a tight t-shirt that she usually loved but suddenly hated. Khadijah knew it showed off the shape of her body. What if her tight shirt made Damon think she wanted him to look at her breast? She wanted to cover up.

Why had it come to this? Why couldn't she go back to Aunt Janice's or the shelter? Why not one of her friends' houses?

Khadijah felt betrayed.

She wanted to go back in time and clean their townhome after school so her mom would feel better. She didn't understand that Jen's addiction and depression was bigger than a bad day. Khadijah didn't mind plastic spoons or sardines for dinner at that moment.

She now had to use all of her courage to get out of that Chevy Cavalier and face the monster that stole her innocence. Fearfully, she got out of the car and followed her mother and Hasaan to the door.

Khadijah almost peed on herself when the door opened.

Chapter 8
On the Table

In Khadijah's mind, she pictured Aunt Kathy to be a big, mean, evil witch. Khadijah had not seen her aunt in years and somewhat blamed her for what Damon did. Khadijah's last memory of her aunt was from the perspective of a molested and afraid child. Jen cut off all ties with Aunt Kathy, so Khadijah's assumption was that she never cared. And even if she did, she never fought to tell Khadijah that she did. The few times Khadijah asked about her Aunt Kathy, Jen would brush her off and change the subject.

Khadijah imagined that when Aunt Kathy opened the door she would be tall and fat with a permanent frown. She imagined her aunt would resemble a street Madam with a bad weave and cigarette hanging from her lips. She conjured up the idea that Damon was sexually deviant because his mother either showed him how to be or subjected him to that type of environment.

Khadijah started to tremble. She wondered if she should start preparing herself to be raped again. She thought entertaining the trauma would make it less jarring and harmful. Khadijah wondered what Damon looked like as well. Khadijah pictured Damon as a tall, dark skinned black thug. She was afraid he would have plans for her as soon as he laid eyes on her pubescent body.

Khadijah snapped out of her thoughts and paid attention to who was truly about to open the door as she heard footsteps behind it.

As Aunt Kathy opened her screen door, tears welled up in her eyes as she looked at her frail, baby sister and her beloved niece and nephew.

"Jesus! Oh Jen! Come on in. I'm so glad to see you honey," Kathy cried in relief.

Jen began to cry as well. She had so much animosity built up towards her sister, but they had the same mother. They were blood and that had to count for something. Kathy then grabbed Hasaan and held him so tight. "You've gotten soooo big, nephew!" She beamed.

“Thanks, Aunt Kathy,” he replied, gratefully.

Kathy finally looked at Khadijah and felt so many emotions. Khadijah looked into her aunt’s eyes. Instead of seeing fear and defeat, she saw hope and familiarity.

Aunt Kathy was older so she had a few grey hairs and kept her hair secured back in a ponytail. Her skin was smooth and the color of milk chocolate. She had honest eyes and pretty teeth. Her voice was warm. She wasn't glamorous like Jen, but she was responsible. That meant something for Khadijah since stability was something she missed.

"Look at how much you've grown, give your auntie a big hug," Aunt Kathy beamed.

Khadijah reached out and hugged her aunt. The embrace was so warm. No one understands how much a child needs their village. To hug someone of her blood was so liberating.

"You're so pretty, Khadijah!" Aunt Kathy said as she kept hugging and kissing her niece and nephew. She hugged them so much her perfume began to rub off on their clothes. She stared at them with so much adoration. They were beautiful blessings. She missed them so much.

It was a lot of love; a lot of missed love, a lot of needed love.

"Thank you, Aunt Kathy! You are very beautiful!" Khadijah complimented. "Could I use your restroom, Auntie?"

Aunt Kathy replied, "Sure, I think Damon is finished in there..."

Khadijah changed her mind and decided to sit down on the love seat. Just as she was squatting down to sit, in walked a tall, dark skinned obese man. He donned a red ball cap, a red and white polo style shirt, black jeans, and red and white tennis. He smelled of strong cologne with a hint of smoke as if he was just at a bar.

All these years Khadijah viewed Jen as her protector, but as she looked over at her mother for validation, all that was left was an emaciated, tired, and defenseless version of her mother. Khadijah realized then that she needed to suck it up and trust the universe to get her through this.

"Damon!" Jen squealed as she embraced her nephew. He hugged his aunt tightly as a look of remorse and regret filled his eyes. He was 24 now. Old enough to reflect on his mistakes, but young enough to carry shame.

"What's up, Hasaan?" He slapped hands with his little cousin and pulled him in for a hood hug. Hasaan hugged Damon back. He did it happily, too. He had no idea this man had raped his big sister. He was just relieved to be around a family member that was a man.

Damon laid eyes on Khadijah for the first time since he'd come into the room. Khadijah used her inner strength to nod at him in greeting.

"Hey Khadijah, how have you been?"

"How do you think I been since you stole my innocence and destroyed my family, you bastard? Oh, by the way, my mom is strung out now from the lack of support," is what Khadijah wanted to say.

Instead she answered, "...Good."

Damon's eyes seemed apologetic. He was genuinely concerned about all that his little cousins were going through. However, without a verbal apology there couldn't be reconciliation. Khadijah was extremely nervous to be sleeping in the same house as him.

They got settled in a guest room and as a family they all ate dinner together. Khadijah began to think about what her mother told her about needing help. What did that mean? Was she staying or leaving?

After dinner, Khadijah and Hasaan showered, got on their pajamas, and told their aunt and mother goodnight.

While Jen thought that her children were asleep, Khadijah was just laying there with her eyes open. Although she felt more comfortable, she was still sleeping somewhere unfamiliar. This transition was a lot different than the others.

She overheard a conversation between her mother and Aunt Kathy sitting in the kitchen. Aunt Kathy was crying again.

"How long do you think you'll be gone? Do the kids even know?" she asked concerned, but annoyed.

"I don't know. I just have to get myself together. I'm gonna check myself in, but first I have to get some things together, you know. Khadijah knows...I told her."

"Well, just keep that element away from here. These kids have been through enough, Jen."

Jen snapped, "I know what my children have been through! If y'all didn't turn your back on us, things would've be better. I raised my fucking kids by my damn self. Y'all milked me dry when I was in the salon and bringing in all that money and now you want to make me feel unwelcomed." her voice and body were shaky.

Aunt Kathy rebutted, "Who is y'all?"

Jen stood up. "All my siblings, you included and even mama! Y'all let Alex beat my ass and then when your son molested my child, y'all didn't even try to be a family." Her eyes filled with tears as she continued. "I'm the youngest, Kathy. I needed y'all, especially when Mama died."

Aunt Kathy stood up. "Jen you always shut down and run whenever anything happens. Ain't nobody finna kiss your ass. We not perfect and neither are you. Look at yourself. Just because you haven't dealt with your past doesn't mean these kids have to suffer with you. You talking about what Khadijah went through, but you pressed charges before you even came to me. At this point I'm trying to be here for these kids so you can get your nose clean. You should be grateful I'm even opening my door to you."

Aunt Kathy's words stung Jen and they hurt because some of it was true. Jen was frustrated and embarrassed. She felt her sister was rubbing her addiction in her face.

Khadijah listened and cried silently. She was glad her aunt was standing up for her and her brother. She felt herself resenting her mother even more. Khadijah cried herself to sleep.

When she woke up, she smelled bacon. Aunt Kathy was making breakfast. Jen was gone and neither Khadijah nor Hasaan asked about their mother's whereabouts. They just wanted to exist and be kids for at least a day.

What Khadijah didn't know was that Jen had signed a power of attorney to relinquish her parental rights temporarily to Aunt Kathy. They would not see her mother for a year.

Chapter 9
Stride Right?

After a big, delicious breakfast with pancakes, scrambled eggs with cheese, pork bacon, sausage, hash browns, and fruit, love radiated through Aunt Kathy's house.

Khadijah began to wonder why her mom never reconciled with her sister until now? She understood how traumatizing it may have been for her. Her daughter was raped and her family was not there to support them. If Khadijah could find it in her heart to forgive, why couldn't her mother?

She wanted to ask her, but Jen wasn't there. It was two in the afternoon and for the first time that day, Khadijah wondered where her mother was. She walked into Aunt Kathy's bedroom and asked.

"Aunt Kathy, where's my mom?"

Aunt Kathy brushed Khadijah off. "I'm sure she'll be here soon. Hasaan said you all wanted to see some old pictures. I have some from your mom and dad's wedding," she said, purposely changing the subject.

Aunt Kathy pulled out a large framed, off white photo album. It had torn plastic and smelled of moth balls. She sat in the middle of the bed and Hasaan and Khadijah sat on each side of her. She opened the makeshift time capsule and unlocked a very big piece of Khadijah's heart.

Family.

Aunt Kathy had pictures of their maternal grandmother who passed away five years ago. All of the pictures seemed like a distant memory. Pictures of Jen as a baby, kid, and teen were in there, too. Seeing her mother with her siblings in the pictures was so beautiful. Khadijah had always seen her mother as a loner outside of a few best friends.

There were pictures of aunts, uncles, cousins, greats, and of major events in the family. Khadijah also noticed resemblances between herself and her blood family. She felt pride at first, but in rushed resentment.

Why had she felt so alone in life with all of this so called family? Why had she seen the walls of a shelter? Why weren't they at her orchestra concerts, dance performances, or spelling bees? They knew her mom didn't celebrate Christmas, so why didn't they at least come pick her and Hasaan up so they could feel included in this so called family?

Khadijah began to cry and ran into her temporary room to lay down.

Hasaan at the time was only 11. Only God knows how all of this trauma was affecting him. He asked Aunt Kathy if Khadijah was okay. She assured him that she would be. Without asking, she knew how her niece may have felt. Aunt Kathy was so grateful to have her niece and nephew. She always felt her sister didn't deserve her children. Aunt Kathy wanted them to feel loved and begin to see that the reason that she hadn't been around was all Jen's fault.

A few months passed and Khadijah finished 8th grade, surviving a partial semester in a city school. Jen was still missing. She didn't even make it to Khadijah's 8th grade graduation ceremony. Aunt Kathy proudly stood in her absence. She took all the credit as the 8th grade teachers praised Khadijah's good behavior and impressive academics.

Khadijah looked unrecognizable from the girl she was before moving. Aunt Kathy took her to a hair salon to get a relaxer and a wrap with a part on the side.

"This is how a young lady should look. You need a perm for that thick stuff."

Khadijah wanted to correct her aunt and remind her that a perm and a relaxer were two different processes, but she let it go. As the daughter of a beautician, she was very knowledgeable about hair care. Khadijah was upset that her aunt relaxed her hair after it had grown out so healthy in its natural state, but hey, she was surviving. A stable home, food on the table, her own room, clothes, and a soon-to-be first Christmas. Can't beat that with a stick.

Damon was never there and if he was, he was cool. He gave Khadijah and Hasaan rides sometimes and brought them snacks. He was like a big brother.

The most exciting part of the summer before high school was Khadijah starting her first job. Since Aunt Kathy was on disability, she qualified to work at 14 with a permit. She was accepted into a program called ArtHands that allowed teens with strong artistic skills to work as artists and get paid. Khadijah chose the dance position.

At her new job she made friends easily and she made her own money. All of her pain was evaporating.

One day, Khadijah spoke on the phone with one of her best friends that she missed so much. She hadn't seen Jackie since a few months after her and her family were evicted. She missed Jackie's family. Her family was Khadijah's family. Also, Kanesha and Jackie were neighbors so if she could get to Jackie, she could get Kanesha.

They were overdue for mischief and boy chasing.

However, Aunt Kathy had her on a leash. She was so strict and up until now Khadijah didn't mind because survival had been most important to her.

While on the call with Jackie, they came up with a great reunion sleepover idea. Khadijah could spend the night over the weekend and go to church with them, just like old times. After she got off the phone, she went downstairs to the living room to ask Aunt Kathy.

"Hey Auntie, I just got off of the phone with Jackie. Can I spend the weekend at their house?"

"I don't know her or her family that well, Khadijah and I don't have gas to drive to the county," Aunt Kathy said, irritated.

"Pops will pick me up," Khadijah pleaded. "He said you don't have to send me with food or anything."

"I don't know them!" Aunt Kathy yelled. "And who is Pops?"

"That's Jackie's dad. He's always been like a dad to me," Khadijah defended. Aunt Kathy was showing a side of herself that

Khadijah had not quite seen before. She was possessive and controlling.

"Well, I don't know him and why is he so willing to come get a 14-year-old girl to spend the night at his house? You would think you would be careful of the situations you put yourself in, Khadijah. You are too trusting. You have breast and you're not the skinniest. Your mother may have let you run around all willy nilly, but not me."

Khadijah turned to walk away in disappointment.

"Get back in here!"she continued, "Don't walk away from me without saying yes ma'am. You are ungrateful and disrespectful just like your mama. Get over here and hold out your hand. I know y'all mama didn't believe in whooping y'all, but she ain't here!"

Aunt Kathy grabbed the wooden back scratcher and repeatedly struck Khadijah's hands and arms. Khadijah watched welts form on her skin. She was more pained by the mistreatment than the physical pain. She actually invited physical pain. Something about it made her feel better about everything she was going through. It gave her a similar high as the one she felt when she masturbated. Any feeling to escape all of her mental pain was welcomed.

She zoned out and cried as Aunt Kathy finished giving her a beating and yelled at her. She composed herself enough to walk upstairs to her room.

Hasaan walked in and sat beside Khadijah on her bed. He hugged his sister and empathized with her. He admitted that earlier that week, Aunt Kathy hit him with a paint stick for eating too much food. It was just starting to seem like they were getting somewhere. It felt like all their problems were beginning to go away...just to find out that Aunt Kathy was Dr. Jekyll/Mrs. Hyde. They missed their mom. In that moment, even with all of their basic needs met, they felt alone and hopeless.

All of a sudden the house phone rang.

"Khadijah and Hasaan, can you come downstairs please?" Aunt Kathy yelled.

They looked at each other with worry in their eyes. They grabbed each other's hands and walked down the stairs together.

Chapter 10
Crawl

Hasaan walked in front of Khadijah as they went down the steps. Khadijah held her arm to protect it, just in case Aunt Kathy was the type to keep going when upset. Instead, Aunt Kathy had remorse and sadness in her eyes.

"Have a seat," she said, pointing to the couch. Aunt Kathy had 2 pills in her hand and a glass of water. She threw them back like candy and chased them with her water. Aunt Kathy often took pills, claiming they were for the pinched nerve in her arm. Khadijah wondered why she needed a book of prescriptions just for a pinched nerve. She had at least 12 medications in a black patent leather pouch that she kept close to her at all times.

The suspense was killing her as to why Aunt Kathy called them downstairs, but with the way she flipped out, Khadijah didn't even want to ask.

"Your mother just called," Aunt Kathy said, in a regretful tone. "She said she would speak with you all soon, but wanted you to know where she was."

Relieved, Khadijah and Hasaan began to cry. They cried because they missed their mom. They had never been away from her for more than a weekend and it had been 7 whole months since they'd last seen her. Khadijah didn't even know how to cope with her being gone. She started telling her friends at school that her mom died because she didn't want to face the fact that she was abandoned.

"Jen...I mean, your mom is in a rehab facility for addiction. They are helping her get back on her feet. She eventually wants to get you all back into her custody." Aunt Kathy lowered her head in shame. "I know I'm different than your mom, but I love you both so much. If she loved you as much as I did she wouldn't have left you."

Khadijah and Hasaan locked eyes and spoke to each other without saying a word. They realized at the moment that Aunt Kathy was sociopathic. The best way to deal with her was to agree with everything she said, behave in a way she approved, and kiss up to survive in her house. They would do so just to survive long enough to make it back to their mom.

They were not in agreement of how she felt, but they played along so they could at least have peace. To help convince Aunt Kathy of their sympathy, they both hugged her.

Khadijah went upstairs and played all of her favorite music to celebrate and contemplate what it would be like to have her identity back. She envisioned herself with natural hair again, trying out different trends of clothes that Aunt Kathy forbid her to wear, experimenting with makeup, and just being Khadijah. She fell asleep with Jill Scott's Words and Sounds Vol. 1 album on repeat.

As fall snuck into their lives, Khadijah started high school. She wore a uniform for the first time and was so excited. She hand selected all of her supplies to match her favorite colors. She also got a rolling book bag since she would have more homework. She always saw how many books high schoolers had and wanted to be prepared.

She didn't realize there was a difference in county high schools and city high schools. For the majority of Khadijah's life, she went to school with all races of people. Even though she experienced a slight culture shock being in an all black environment for 8th grade, it was still a small school so she figured she would be in an integrated environment again for high school. When she walked through the doors of St. Ville High School, her mind was blown.

Instantly, she noticed the uniform she so carefully ironed was a joke. No one else abided by the dress code. They had on the school shirt but instead of traditional uniform pants like the ones on the uniform policy, girls had on low rise, tight hip hugger khakis. They rocked fancy jackets to hide the shirts so they could appear to dress in plain clothes. The boys had on sagging name brand khakis and the school shirts untucked. They had gold mouthpieces and gold chains. All black students. They seemed so much taller and more mature.

Khadijah followed the directions on her schedule and made it to the freshmen hallway. There she found other lost and surprised freshmen that dressed by the book and were eager to find their classes. Khadijah also noticed how good looking the boys were. However, she wouldn't entertain them because she knew how crazy her aunt was. She figured she'd holla at them next year once she lived back with her mom.

Khadijah fell into the groove of this new adventure called high school. She made friends easily. Outside of one time when she was made fun of for wearing an actual book bag, she fit right in. She also got along well with the upperclassmen.

Khadijah played along by her aunt's rules and stayed focused. The only thing she entertained outside of her academics was the makeshift drama club the school created and the school's choir.

Jen called in two-week increments at first. Then once a week and eventually once a day. She worked diligently to rebuild trust with her children.

As the seasons changed, Christmas was approaching. The facility that Jen stayed at was rewarding the women who continued their path to sobriety with home visits. That was the best Christmas gift Khadijah and Hasaan could ask for, even though Aunt Kathy was already planning a huge Christmas. Khadijah overheard her aunt on the phone several times talking to her friends.

"These kids deserve a proper Christmas. I don't know why she had to deny these kids of that. Mama always gave us a great, big Christmas."

Khadijah understood her mother's beliefs, but she admired Christmas every year. She couldn't wait to see what all the hoopla was about. Although Jen didn't celebrate Christmas with her kids, they grew up celebrating Kwanzaa. She also gifted her children all year round and threw them the most extravagant parties for their birthdays. Khadijah never truly appreciated these things until she went without them.

The day came where Khadijah and Hassaan could go visit their mother after almost a year had passed. Aunt Kathy made sure she dressed them very nicely, bundled them up in their coats, and got into Aunt Kathy's red Toyota. They drove for about 25 minutes. The place where Jen lived was in the county, too. Khadijah realized the county didn't seem as familiar anymore. It had been 2 years since they were evicted from their luxury townhome. That life wasn't hers anymore.

When they arrived at the convent, a nun greeted them and took their coats. Inside was a very warm, homelike center. She led them past a common area, the chapel, and the kitchen. It felt like forever until Khadijah could see her mother. As she looked around, staring at other women being reunited with their families, she heard her voice.

"My babies are here!" Jen squealed.

Khadijah turned her head towards the sound of her mother's voice so instinctively. Almost reminiscent of a newborn when they hear their mother's voice for the first time. As she turned her head, Khadijah felt butterflies in her stomach as her favorite person in the world walked toward her. Even after crack, homelessness, and defeat, Jen was still beautiful. This curse of addiction had not won.

Jen had on flare jeans and a mock neck sweater. She had her long, wavy hair brushed back into a low bun. The grey hair that she fought to cover with color years prior was invading the crown of her head. Her skin was the lightest brown it had ever been. Clearly she hadn't been vacationing all this time. Jen was so tiny. She wasn't as skinny as before but, in comparison to Khadijah's pubescent body, she was very frail. Tears of joy were in her eyes.

As Hassaan and Khadijah hugged their mother it felt like the world stopped. They all hugged for a good two minutes before Jen reached out to hug her sister. Only God knows what went through Aunt Kathy's mind at that moment. She smiled warmly. No tears, just a smile.

"Would you all like a tour?" Jen asked. Of course, they all obliged.

Jen led them around the fascinating facility. Khadijah admired the organization who sponsored the house. Each woman had their own room. They also learned more about the program. After each woman mastered a healthy schedule of prayer, affirmations, eating clean, exercise, single and group therapy, and healthy recreation, they are allowed to leave the premises and come back by curfew. This extension of rehab aided in allowing addicts a realistic way to recovery. After their tour, they all sat down for a meal.

"Khadijah, you're turning into a woman," Jen beamed. "You're so pretty! Did you relax your hair?"

"Actually, I got her hair relaxed," Aunt Kathy jumped in. "She needed something manageable for school."

Jen grinded her teeth but played it off. She recognized how bossy and intimidating her sister could be. She wanted to question her children about how they've been treated and how they really felt. She also didn't want to seem ungrateful for her sister being there for her.

"Sister Jude paired us with a therapist. Khadijah, I don't know if you remember Dr. Thomas, but she recommends we start our family therapy. It's important that we all heal together. It's also a way for us all to share our feelings."

"That sounds nice," Aunt Kathy said, smiling.

As if she was competing, Khadijah threw her hand up. "I'm in!" she said. Hassaan just nodded.

After they bantered, laughed, and shared stories the sun started to go down and Jen's eyes began to water. Khadijah and Hasaan's followed. They knew their visiting time had come to an end.

As they got their coats on, Khadijah felt her stomach drop. She wanted to stay. She hadn't felt so loved and so comfortable in so long. It was conflicting. Aunt Kathy made sure their physical needs were met, but those things didn't equate to love.

Jen hugged her family and watched them get into the car and drive off. Intuition told her that she had no room to fall off again. This was it. She was determined to be with her children again. Jen was willing to face all of her issues head on just to be reunited with them.

Chapter 11
Walk

Aunt Kathy knew after that visit, her days with her niece and nephew were numbered. Yes, Jen fell, but as always she recovered and would persevere. Aunt Kathy pulled out all the stops for Christmas. Since they'd never officially had a Christmas, Khadijah and Hasaan were grateful for her effort. She bought a big, beautiful Christmas tree, wrapped all the gifts, cooked a large dinner, and played Christmas music.

Still, their focus was on reuniting with their mother.

Winter faded away and spring came.

Khadijah neared the end of her first year of high school. She made it through with no fights, no drama, and maintained a 4.0 GPA. She really had no choice though. Once she discovered that crazy side of her aunt, she didn't want to push her.

Jen was down to her last four weeks at the recovery house and after completion of her program, she would receive an apartment voucher and job leads so she could transition back into the real world. Several home visits and mini field trips happened throughout those remaining months between Jen and her children. All of them "supervised" by Aunt Kathy.

Aunt Kathy began to grow even more jealous of her sister. First, she envied Jen for her birth order, then her skin being lighter, and then her hair being straighter. She was envious of Jen being loved more by family. Even after becoming a crackhead and losing everything, her children still adored her. Aunt Kathy's childish mind didn't understand unconditional love. She clearly hadn't read the bible like she said she did.

A part of Jen's healing required that her, her children, and her sister all have therapy to be sure everyone had understanding and wouldn't harbor the hurt feelings from Jen's addiction. The therapist they met with was Dr. Shanice Gorman. Dr. Gorman was a black woman very well versed on the issues that plague black families.

After everyone introduced themselves, she started the session by asking everyone how they felt about reuniting. Aunt Kathy spoke first.

"Well, I'm very happy for my sister. However, I am concerned about the safety of my niece and nephew. Jen puts on a good poker face, but people relapse everyday."

"It's important that we use "I" statements and be less pessimistic about your sister's recovery," Dr. Gorman said before Aunt Kathy could continue. Jen looked at Aunt Kathy angrily, but grateful for Dr. Gorman's mediation.

"I'm very excited to be back with my mom," Khadijah said. "I'm thankful for my aunt but I belong with my mom...my mom lets me be who I am. I feel like my aunt tries to control me to be what she wants…"

"No, little girl you want to be grown like your mom and I won't let you," Aunt Kathy snapped. "And you're being disrespectful!"

"Sharing her feelings isn't being disrespectful," Dr. Gorman explained. "She's 15 and in the middle of a very delicate transition. It's important that her feelings are present."

Aunt Kathy stood up. "It's very clear that this meeting isn't going to good well because you are friends with Jen. She always lures people in to like her more. I never stood a chance. I'm leaving now. Come on kids!"

Khadijah looked at Hasaan. He never even got a chance to share his feelings. They gave their mom a hug and started to cry. Jen cried silently. She refused to ruin her chances of reuniting with her children. After Aunt Kathy ruined the therapy session, Dr. Gorman gave Jen very serious advice.

"Jen, you must continue on your path of sobriety. Those children are in a toxic environment. She is ruining their confidence and character. You must get your kids back."

Jen got into full soldier mode. Her mind was made up. Just like she braved her escape from her abusive marriage, she would overcome this.

When Aunt Kathy got home, she yelled at the children to go to their rooms. She knew deep inside she couldn't discipline Khadijah for what she said in therapy. She was just hurt. She was doing the best she could with them and they still wanted to go with their mom.

Her friend was coming over so she wanted to straighten up. However, she couldn't help but feel vengeful. She felt that Khadijah made her look bad in front of that therapist. She felt as if Khadijah was picking up where her mother left off. Aunt Kathy called Khadijah downstairs. She came down stairs with burdens all over her face and puffy eyes to match. Aunt Kathy asked Khadijah to sit down.

"Niece, I need to ask you something I've wanted to ask you for a long time..."

"Yes, ma'am?" Khadijah asked, already irritated by her aunt's manipulative spirit.

"Did your mother make you say my Damon did those things to you?"

Khadijah was stunned. She had used all of her strength and control to live harmoniously under the same roof as her rapist. She was finally feeling forgiveness in her heart and now her aunt had the audacity to question her. As the trauma surfaced in her mind, tears began to well up in her tired eyes again.

"No. It did happen to me."

"I was never gone long enough for him to do that to you. Are you sure it wasn't another family member?"

"I was old enough to know who hurt me and how they did it!" Khadijah defended herself. She wanted to body slam her aunt right then and there. She'd had enough of her and her evil ways.

"...Your mom took you away so I didn't get a chance to question you. I'm only asking because I should have had the chance to question you, too," Aunt Kathy pleaded as she made excuses for her insensitivity.

"The authorities questioned me. They also gave me a rape kit," Khadijah explained. "I was a child."

The doorbell rang. It was Jean, Aunt Kathy's friend. Jean was very honest and bold. She was much older than Aunt Kathy, but she was the balance Aunt Kathy needed.

Jean walked in, unstable due to her cane, and fell onto the couch. "What's going on? I can cut the tension in this room with a knife."

"Well, I decided to ask Khadijah what I been wanting to know," Aunt Kathy said.

"Kathy, didn't this baby just have therapy with her mama about her abandoning them? What the hell is wrong with you? I told you not to ask her that!" Jean fussed, unapologetically. She had a very honest relationship with Aunt Kathy and always said it like it was.

Khadijah cried harder. For once, someone understood and verbalized how she felt. However, she was not prepared for what would come out of Jean's mouth next.

"I told your Aunt Kathy that Damon told me that he was molesting you. He was very upset and sad by what he had done. When I tried to tell Kathy, she got mad at me and kicked me out of her house."

Khadijah couldn't handle it any more. She ran out of the living room and ran straight into Damon. He was so tall and so big. She looked up at him in fear and ran around him up the stairs and to her room. She laid on the bed face first into the pillows. For the first time, Khadijah wanted to die. She couldn't handle all of this anymore. She began to tell herself that her life wasn't valuable. A black cloud began to invade her mind.

Something familiar, yet distant sat on the bed with Khadijah. It was a strong, familiar presence. Khadijah wondered if it was God?

The hairs on her arms began to stand up. Her breathing became deep. Her heart rate became a steady drum. Khadijah had recently heard a popular song called, "I Need You Now." It was different than the gospel songs she had heard before. This song was a full on testimony of how she felt. She especially loved how the singer didn't use any background singers or a choir. In that moment, with the presence of God, Khadijah heard that song. There wasn't a CD player or radio on but she heard it.

God sat on that bed and comforted Khadijah in a way that she yearned for her whole life. She laid down on her bed and God tucked her in. He rubbed her back and gave her rest. He renewed her mind and in the middle of all the tragedy He assured her everything would be okay. God rocked Khadijah to sleep. She couldn't tell if what she was feeling was metaphorical or literal. All she knew was that it was real. Khadijah had experienced the power of God. He was equipped to end all of the curses that were present in her life.

In the next few days, Khadijah soaked in positivity and gospel songs. Khadijah and Hasaan also began to pack their belongings over the course of the next week.

Jen was ready for the big move two weeks early. The reunion was supposed to feel big and grand, however it was short and sweet. Khadijah and Hasaan only had their beds and small furniture. Jen lost everything in storage so outside of what the nuns donated, she just had an air mattress and a fan.

The apartment she was awarded was in the hood and simple, but they were together and picked up right where they left off. Jen was a stronger version of herself and was grateful to have her kids. They would finish off the summer catching up and preparing for the next school year. Hasaan was so quiet through most of the transition. Khadijah worried about him, but trusted God to connect with him as He did her.

In the fall, Khadijah returned to school different than the previous year. Her hair was the way she wanted it with weave, accessories, and even some makeup. Jen believed children needed room to be themselves. She also felt so bad for what she put them through. She overcompensated and had a hard time saying no.

Khadijah was more relaxed at school and decided to join the majorette team. It was so exhilarating to use her physical body to perform. She also loved the attention she started to get from boys. The drumline and band played for the majorettes as they danced in barely there uniforms. The drumline in particular drooled over the

Villesettes. One drummer in particular always stared Khadijah down. His name was Marcus. Marcus secretly had a crush on Khadijah. Even though he was handsome, tall, and sweet, he wasn't Khadijah's type.

Khadijah wanted a bad boy. She had a taste for trouble. The good girl act she had to keep up all last year was coming to an end.

She spent the entire school year exploring and finding herself. Jen found a better apartment that they moved to which made it even easier for Khadijah to host sleepovers. It was still in the hood, but a nicer part. Khadijah would have friends over even when her mother wasn't there. She was like a wild tiger that had been released from her cage in a zoo.

Khadijah traveled with her dance team, made new friends, reconnected with old friends, and let her grades slip. By the time she turned 16, she had about 5 different boyfriends, smoked weed, drank liquor, and added a one night stand to her sex count.

Jen knew deep inside that Khadijah was spiraling out of control but she didn't want her daughter feeling controlled or sad. She wanted to make it up to her for being gone. Jen enabled Khadijah by keeping her in fly clothes, banging hairstyles, and giving her permission to do what she wanted. Khadijah somehow stayed respectful and kind. The skill of manipulation that she mastered long ago was now being used to get what she wanted out of life.

Khadijah got a job at the end of the school year at a clothing store. She dedicated her whole summer to getting money. Jen was still struggling to get on her feet. They didn't have a car so Khadijah felt if she would be on a bus, at least she would be fly.

Summer and its escapades came and went. Khadijah decided that for her junior year she would slow down a little. The first day of school, she showed up with bright red natural hair and denim outerwear to mask her uniform. Her mere presence was a whole mood. She had been listening to a lot of Erykah Badu and Jeezy, so she was sensual and on a mission. There was a new boy at school. He was a senior and he was fine!

Khadijah never dated any boys at her school. Even in her loosest moments, county boys had her heart. She still loved bad boys, but the bad boys at her school were beyond bad. This new boy had just the right balance of prep and hood. He was clean cut and smelled like heaven. His name was Jose.

She always looked him in his eyes in passing but figured since he was a senior, he was out of her league. At the end of the day, Khadijah went to her locker and there he was, almost as if he was waiting on her. They locked eyes and made a connection right away.

Jose was 6 feet even. He had the smoothest dark chocolate skin, perfect white teeth, and wore his hair in a low cut with waves. He smelled like heaven and had a voice so deep it rattled. He had car keys in his hand as he asked for her number. She never dated a guy with his own car before. Khadijah told Jose that she caught the bus home and he offered her a ride. She knew that she should probably ask permission first but oh well, her mom would understand.

Khadijah walked outside of school with Jose feeling so proud to have bagged the new boy with little effort. She was proud to be seen getting into his car. He was so mature and grown compared to other boys she dated.

Jose turned his ignition on and the rumble of the 2004 Monte Carlo felt so good. She looked out of the window and felt a colony of butterflies setting up inside of her stomach.

Chapter 12
Run

Rides home from school with Jose turned into long talks in the car. That turned into dates, meeting mothers, friends and family. Before long, Khadijah and Jose were an item. They walked around like black Barbie and Ken.

Khadijah was 16, slim thick, and full of life. She was loved by many because of her unique spirit and down to earth personality. She was so excited to have a boyfriend that matched her fly. She started listening to love songs frequently and doodled "Jose and Khadijah" over everything.

Jen was a little concerned by how infatuated Khadijah was with Jose. However, with her only being two years sober, she was still trying to regain her daughter's trust. Khadijah and Jen had a very open relationship. They talked about everything. Jen even told Khadijah to come to her when she thought she was ready to have sex. Jen wanted to make sure she had the proper birth control. By the spring of her junior year, Khadijah told Jen that she was ready.

Jen ordered a cab and took her daughter to a popular family planning facility. There were signs up all over the clinic about different birth control. They signed in and asked Khadijah to go urinate in a plastic cup before she was called back. She complied. As she balanced the cup with the flow of her urine, she noticed an unfamiliar smell. It smelled like vitamins and made her feel a little queasy. This was the third time she'd felt like that in a few months. She put her name on the label, stuck it to the cup, and placed it in a basket where the staff would retrieve it and test it for pregnancy.

Khadijah went back to the waiting room with her mom and waited to be called. They eventually called Khadijah's name.

"Are you giving your mother permission to be in the room with you and the doctor?" the nurse asked.

Confused, Khadijah looked at her mother and nodded her head. As they got settled into the room, the nurse asked Khadijah when was her last period. She really couldn't remember, but deep down inside she didn't want them to ask about sex. Khadijah had been having unprotected sex with Jose since homecoming and they did it often. He told her that he didn't like condoms and that he didn't have any STDs. She believed him. Jose also told her the pull out method was better than condoms.

"I don't know how to say this Khadijah, but you're pregnant," the nurse said. "We don't know how far along you are but we can schedule another appointment with you after you discuss your choices with your partner."

Khadijah sank down into her chair, so afraid and embarrassed. Jose lied to her.

"How many weeks can she be if she decides to terminate?" Jen had tears in her eyes but was serious about helping her daughter. Khadijah heard of abortions and saw girls her age with babies. She didn't want to deal with either. She really wanted to tell Jose but she couldn't at that time. After the appointment, Jen was disappointed but instead of scolding Khadijah, she assured her that the situation would be okay.

Khadijah felt like she betrayed her mother. She didn't want her to feel the need to relapse. That night, she overheard her on the phone with her sponsor. She usually called her for needed strength. When Khadijah called Jose to tell him, he was surprised and scared. He rushed her off of the phone, which was weird, but Khadijah was tired so she didn't stress it.

She rubbed her stomach in a circular motion. She didn't have much to give a child so she was leaning towards getting an abortion. Within a week, Khadijah had an ultrasound appointment. They determined that she was 12 weeks. State law allowed abortions up to 14 weeks. The abortion would cost $750 and she was running out of time. Jose kept saying he would tell his mother, but he never did. By the time he told his mom the abortion was already paid for and he changed the narrative. He told his mother that he wanted the baby but he respected Khadijah's choice. That was a lie. He was relieved when he found out she wanted to terminate.

A week passed and Jen found some way to come up with $750. Khadijah and Jen caught a cab to the family planning facility. As they pulled into the lot, protestors were outside with picket signs and images of ripped apart fetuses.

"Murderer!" they screamed at the car.

Khadijah felt scared and guilty. She wondered if her baby had eyes, arms, legs, and a face. They signed in and sat in the waiting area. The packet they received at the ultrasound appointment said the abortion would be a 3-hour procedure.

Someone finally called Khadijah's name to pee in a cup again. Next, they had her speak with a therapist just to make sure her choice was solid and her mentality was clear. After that, they had her change into a hospital gown, assigning her a locker to put her belongings. The nurse gave her a pill sedative to calm her nerves but it barely worked. Khadijah was terrified.

She felt her stomach and noticed it was firm at the bottom. That was obviously the baby. They gave her an ultrasound before the procedure to make sure it was still alive. Khadijah asked if it was possible for her to get a picture. The staff thought it was weird but gave her one anyway.

After they printed out the blurry ultrasound picture, Khadijah was sent to sit by 4 other ladies that had on identical hospital gowns and footies as hers. She usually spoke but this was not a social gathering. One by one they went behind the large white door. Each time she heard a loud vacuum and a cry of pain. She was afraid but she didn't want to waste her mother's money. For the first time, Khadijah realized how selfish Jose was. He should have been there with her. His mom had lots of money, so why didn't she offer to help with this nightmare.

"Khadijah?" the nurse called.

Khadijah raised her hand like a kid in school being called on. The nurse led her to the room behind the large white door where there was a white man with glasses and wrinkled skin. The nurse told Khadijah that she would hold her hand and be there for the whole procedure. The doctor started with a speculum that he slid inside of Khadijah to open her up.

"Ouch," Khadijah squirmed. “That hurts!"

"Your boyfriend must not be very big if that hurt..." the doctor replied.

Khadijah was so embarrassed. How could the doctor make a joke like that? The nurse started to ask Khadijah questions about her personal life to get her mind off of the procedure. Khadijah felt so awkward and afraid. She felt the doctor give her numbing shots in her vagina. Then they turned on that loud vacuum. The nurse broke the meaningless small talk to tell Khadijah she would feel cramping soon.

The vacuum was so strong inside of her. She felt a pull at her pelvis and heard wet gurgling noises. A loud pop and suction happened and then the cramp came. She moaned as she felt the doctor put a diaper like pad on her and walked out of the room. Khadijah began to sob uncontrollably. The nurse stood her up and walked her to the recovery room. There were 8 women on hospital beds and there was an island desk in the middle where the nurses monitored them. They set Khadijah up with a blanket, a cup of juice, and crackers, encouraging her to rest until her bleeding stopped. Khadijah noticed other women and girls in the room who were hooked up to IVs. The sedative got the best of her and the next thing she remembered was walking into her bedroom.

Jose met her and her mom there for support and he brought pizza. Khadijah didn't want any. She cried to Jose. He felt sorry for aiding in Khadijah's current pain. Jen felt so sorry for her daughter but was relieved. She gave Jose permission to spend the night so Khadijah could feel somewhat better.

Weeks and months followed and Khadijah still felt very sad about her abortion. Jose broke up with her but said he still wanted to stay close friends. As the school year ended, she was really so broken that she barely wanted to live. Her self worth had gone down drastically. Khadijah really felt sad to know that Jose's idea of close friends was casual sex without a title. Instead of standing up for herself, she did what any other teenager would do when they felt of little worth. She let him use her when he felt like it.

Khadijah worked, cried, and slept all summer. She was falling deeper and deeper into depression and by the start of her senior year she was run down, tired, depressed, and jealous of Jose being in college. He barely answered her phone calls anymore unless he wanted sex.

Khadijah started to have a familiar queasiness. She also smelled vitamins in her pee. When she got her abortion earlier that year they told her that if she ever needed birth control or testing, she could come without her mother. She made an appointment for a pregnancy test just to ease her mind even though she was on a birth control called the Nufre Ring. It was a method that was new that seemed easier than a daily pill.

Well, that Nufre Ring didn't work. The test revealed she was indeed pregnant again. How embarrassing and dumb she felt. Khadijah caught a bus home and called Jose's number. Her mind was made up. The only logical answer she came up with to solve all of her problems was to commit suicide. At this point in Khadijah's life she let her mom down, Hassaan was embarrassed of her, her friends gossiped about her, and she refused to get another abortion. Her and this baby would just go to heaven together. She was so convinced to kill herself that she wasn't even sad. It was the answer to all of her problems.

Jose answered the phone and Khadijah spoke quickly.

"Hi, Jose. I'm pregnant again. I'm tired and done."

She hung up, turned her phone off, and thought of her mom. At first, Jen would probably be sad but she wouldn't have the burdens Khadijah brought anymore, so she stuck to her plan. A few months ago, Khadijah had a pulled tooth and had a prescription for 650 mg Ibuprofen. She had 8 left and figured if she took all of them at once, it could kill her before anyone got home. She laid in the bed, took all 8 pills with a little water, and waited. Khadijah felt herself getting sleepy.

Suddenly, her door was kicked in. It was EMS and Jose. After he got off the phone with Khadijah he felt something wasn't right and called 911. They gave Khadijah fluids on the ambulance ride and after blood work discovered she was pregnant. Instead of pumping her stomach they force fed her tar. The tar was supposed to induce vomiting that would prevent the medicine from hitting her bloodstream. Khadijah was happy to see Jose, but disappointed that her plan didn't work. Why couldn't she just die in peace?

"I'm sorry I did this to you, Khadijah," Jose cried. "Why would you do this?"

She had no answer for him.

After twenty minutes of consciousness, in walked Jen. A woman working on 3 years of sobriety and feeling every ounce of karma for leaving her children in the past. She was so hurt, but like always she was a soldier. She couldn't help but feel the thick curse of substance abuse. The doctors questioned her over and over outside of the door about Khadijah's access to drugs.

"Did you disperse her medicine or just gave her the bottle?" the doctor asked, judgmentally.

Jen answered carefully, "I monitored her but after her tooth healed, I put the medicine in the cabinet just in case we would need it later."

"Why do you think you would need access to prescription painkillers without a doctor's instruction? Also did you even know that your daughter is pregnant?" the doctor continued to try to discredit Jen.

She told the truth and shamed him in the process, "Look sir. I told you all that happened. You all are not about to hound me for trusting my 17 year old to take her medicine. She made a mistake. She is a happy normal, hormonal teenager who had a bad day. Now let me see my child. Keeping her away from someone who loves her is definitely not helping her right now!"

Jen pushed her way through the door so she could be with Khadijah. She was 17, so she was almost an adult but not quite. She still needed her mother. Jen walked over to the bed and hugged her daughter tightly.

Jen leaned down so that her mouth was level with Khadijah's ear. She lowered her voice so she could privately advise her on how to navigate this situation.

"I love you, baby. I love you so much...I'm sorry about all of this and we will talk later but right now I need you to snap out of this shit. If you don't convince these people that you just had a bad day and you really want to live, they will put you on a 72-hour psych hold. I know you're pregnant and we will handle this together. Please for me, put your big girl panties on so we can get home."

Khadijah heard the desperation in her mother's voice and saw the sincerity in her eyes. Jen was ride or die, right or wrong. Khadijah took her mom's advice and told the case workers and nurses that she wanted to live and was scared about her pregnancy. By the grace of God, they released her to go home.

After an ultrasound appointment, they decided that this baby would live. Khadijah felt guilty for making an attempt on her and her unborn child's life but was grateful for a second chance. She was already three months pregnant. Her baby was due in the spring.

Jose became an afterthought. His opinion wasn't needed going further. Khadijah was determined to finish high school, have her baby, and go to college. She had the support from her mom, a portion of friends, and now a new reason growing inside of her.

Khadijah found out a few months later that she was having a boy.

All of her friends at school spoiled her. They were like her own personal village. They fed her and encouraged her to drink water. Her school was known for fighting and violence but teen pregnancy was so prevalent that they actually had care and resources for teen mothers. The school even had a daycare built into it.

Khadijah's teachers were disappointed once they noticed she was showing. All but one shook their heads in shame. She had one teacher that supported her and assured her that life would still go on even after she had her baby. Her name was Mrs. Klein. Mrs. Klein was five years from retirement, a member of Delta Sigma Theta, and drove a red 2-door convertible to school. Everyone looked up to her. She believed in Khadijah.

The lack of a family presence got to Khadijah sometimes. She didn't have any relationship with blood family outside of her mother and brother. Khadijah feared she couldn't offer her son anything. However, the friends who were like family made up for the loss. Kanesha and Jackie were still close to her. She also made friends with a beautiful girl named Shonte, Tay for short. They met at her summer job.

Tay frequently took Khadijah out to dinner and didn't mind hanging out even though she was pregnant. She bought the baby lots of gifts and was always ready whenever Khadijah had to have a showdown with Jose. Tay joked often that she was Khadijah's baby daddy. Khadijah also made friends with the girls in her support group. The hospital that provided her prenatal care had a teen pregnancy center that focused on health and wellness for teen moms-to-be. They ranged from age 13-18. The group provided free birth classes, gift cards to offset costs, prenatal care, and a doula for the birth.

Eventually, Jose's family acted like they somewhat cared. They even promised to get the baby a bassinet.

Khadijah began nesting. After her homework was completed, she would clean her room and feel her stomach for kicks. At times, she still felt guilty for wanting to die, but as she felt her baby boy's tiny kicks, she was assured that life was such a wonderful thing. Khadijah vowed to never get that dark again. That curse would die instead.

Chapter 13
Groove Back

One of Khadijah's selfless friends threw her a cozy baby shower. She loved the song "Bossy" by Kelis. In the video, she wore a tapered relaxed cut with a long bang, so Khadijah rocked an all white outfit and her new haircut like Kelis'. "Bossy" was her personal soundtrack, it was Khadijah's mood going further. The shower was a success and her baby boy got so many gifts.

The pains she felt in the past would no longer plague her or her unborn baby. She was fierce, mature, and had a made up mind. Khadijah had just got accepted to the local state college with a scholarship for having a high ACT score.

Jose started to fall in love with Khadijah again. He loved her new self-confidence. Sadly, she only entertained him to keep her little family together. She wanted it to work, but if it didn't she would be okay.

She was home often due to being placed on maternity leave. Her due date was really close to her graduation day. Khadijah hoped that her baby would come early enough so she could still make graduation. All but one of her teachers excused her finals. Her Probability and Statistics teacher was not so understanding.

"I'm sorry, but you need this grade to graduate. Please figure out a way to get it completed." She didn't care that Khadijah had a lot on her plate and had been a good student thus far. She was an intolerant, white, pretentious woman who judged Khadijah for being a teen mom.

As Khadijah approached her 37th week of pregnancy, Kanesha came to spend the night at her house so she could hopefully witness the baby's birth. It was cool to hear stories about friends being in the room for the birth. One night before they went to sleep, Khadijah's cat, Egypt, started to meow very loudly. Khadijah shooed her away as she fell asleep. She was awaken by the deepest pain she had ever felt. Her stomach was rock hard and she was convinced that she'd just had a real contraction. Khadijah felt Braxton Hicks weeks prior and even went to the hospital for a false alarm. This was it.

Just as soon as she wrapped her head around the first one, another came at full strength. This was exactly what they described in her birthday class. She was in labor. Khadijah quickly woke Kanesha up.

"I'm having contractions," she said. "I think I'm in labor!"

Kanesha jumped up, happily. Since she had relocated with family for high school, she was excited to be there for the birth. Kanesha went to Jen's room and shook her shoulders.

"Mama Jen, Khadijah is having back to back contractions!"

Jen hopped up and slid on her clothes quickly. They grabbed the hospital bag that had been packed for a month. Jen called Khadijah's other best friends, Jackie and Tay. They agreed to meet at the hospital. She called Jose and he told her that he had to work. Jen wouldn't let his absence discourage her daughter.

When they arrived at the hospital, Khadijah was hooked up to a monitor that read her contractions. Kanesha joked and teased Khadijah as each one approached. Whenever Khadijah buckled in pain, her best friends and mother erupted in laughter. They were making lemonade. Instead of this being a sad event of a teen mom delivering a fatherless child, it turned into a girls' night out. They assigned Khadijah a triage doula until she got admitted into her room. Khadijah felt the pain getting stronger and stronger.

They assigned Khadijah to Room 734. She was a fan of numerology and thought the room number was lucky. After everyone got settled, she requested that her Mariah Carey album get played. She also made a request for an epidural. They assured her that after she dilated to 5 1/2 centimeters that she could get it.

A small, gentle knock followed by a warm voice was at the door. It was India, Khadijah's official birthing doula. India's voice was deep and gentle like Lalah Hathaway. She was brown skinned with back length locs. She was a thick woman and had a bag of goodies and a mission to help Khadijah deliver her baby boy.

While midwives and doctors are concerned about the baby, the doula helps the mother through the birthing process and the initial bonding with the baby. After introducing herself and asking permission to touch, India began to use reflexology massage techniques to mute Khadijah's labor pain. It was like magic. Khadijah almost called off her epidural but since she'd heard rumors about the ring of fire, she decided to proceed. India brought a story book with blank spaces in it for Khadijah to create a birthing story for her son. They joked about Khadijah drifting off and talking in her sleep. India also snuck Khadijah frozen juice, even though she wasn't supposed to have it. India also praised Khadijah's best friends and mother for being in attendance for such a beautiful milestone. She never pointed out Jose's absence, but focused on the positives. Khadijah was healthy and surrounded by love.

After 11 hours of progressive labor, the doctor checked Khadijah's cervix and confirmed she was at 10 cm and it was time to push. Khadijah looked around the room at the doctor, the two nurses, her mother, Kanesha, Jackie, Tay, and India. She was so covered in love. The baby was so covered in love.

As a nurse held one thigh, Tay held the other. Her mom held one hand and Jackie held the other. Kanesha was at the foot of the bed watching as a miracle began to take place. They watched the monitor and awaited the next contraction.

The doctor spoke firmly. "Bare down and 1, 2, 3, 4, 5, 6, 7, 8, 9, 10! Good job...Breathe, breathe! You're doing great, Khadijah. Great pushing for your first baby."

The next contraction came and although the pain was gone, the pressure was intense. Khadijah listened and pushed, this time the whole room joined in on the counting. Khadijah was so bratty that she got mad at her friends and accused them of counting slow. The room erupted with laughter. After 3 more pushes the doctor said, "In 2 more pushes, your baby boy will be here."

Khadijah felt the presence of God just like she felt Him years ago when she was in distress and He reunited her with her mom. She realized her strength and promised God that her childish ways were over. This baby would be raised without her burdens. He would be great and not cursed.

What was supposed to be the last two pushes turned into just one. At 1:22 am on April 21st, 2007, Zahir Amir Jones was born. He came out so fast that the doctor almost dropped him. When they asked who would cut the umbilical cord, Khadijah chose Tay. She stood in for all the emotional support that Khadijah needed, so she deserved it. Baby Zah was light brown with chunky eyes. He was 7 lbs, 3oz and had the softest cry. There wasn't a dry eye in the room. She did it. Khadijah really did it. After years of guilt and mistakes, she did something right.

After the nurses cleaned Zahir up, they placed him on Khadijah's bare chest. Jen was an advocate for breastfeeding so she stood near to support her daughter. The best friends watched anxiously and curiously. As teenagers, they were all taking in so much. India showed Khadijah how to comfortably latch her baby on. Instinctively, Zah latched on and quickly gulped down his first meal. By the time the lactation consultant came by to teach Khadijah how to breastfeed, Zahir had already nursed twice. She instead gave her a few more position tips and congratulated the new mom and family.

Jen stepped into the hall to call Jose. Although she loathed his existence and knew he didn't deserve her daughter, he was still Zahir's father. Jose told Jen that he would try to come to the hospital. As angry as she was by his insensitivity, she wasn't going to ruin her daughter's experience.

After a long nap, they moved Khadijah and Zahir to another room so they could accept visitors. Their first visitor outside of her besties was Mrs. Klein. The horrible teacher that wouldn't waive her final made sure she printed one out for Khadijah to complete. Mrs. Klein brought it to the hospital for Khadijah so that she could be in good standing to graduate next month. So in between breastfeeding, sitz baths for a third degree laceration from pushing and surviving hemorrhoids, she completed her Probability and Statistic final from the hospital bed.

Mrs. Klein proudly put it in a folder to return to the witch teacher. She spent an hour visiting with Khadijah and her new bundle of joy. Night time fell and the visitors left. Jen went home to change clothes.

It was just Khadijah and her baby alone for the first time. She cuddled Zahir, told him how much she loved him, and brushed his hair ever so softly. He was her own personal doll.

Jose showed up an hour before the door was locked for visitors. When he walked in the quality of the room decreased. Khadijah loathed him at this point. He smelled like weed. She asked him to wash his hands before he touched baby Zah. He picked up Zahir and said, "He's a cute little baby."

"Yeah, he is. He's really calm, too," Khadijah said in a monotone voice.

He looked into the newborn's eyes and saw himself. He smiled remorsefully, probably because he felt guilty for not making the birth.

"You should've made him a junior," he joked.

"It would've been nice if you could have made it for the birth," Khadijah hinted.

Jose was mesmerized by Zahir, "Well, I'm here now for my lil nigga."

Jose put his sunglasses on the baby's little face as a joke. The glasses were so big but it was so cute. Khadijah couldn't help but laugh. Jose took out his Blackberry and took a picture. He kissed Khadijah and said he wanted to be a family.

She was relieved and believed him like a naive girl would, even though he couldn't get the bassinet his family promised. Thank God for Tay. She bought it as soon as she found out he wasn't going to come through.

Just when Khadijah had redefined the word family for the greater good, he came to disturb her definition of the word yet again. He was a ticking bomb and was there to do what bombs do. Anticipate, waste time, explode, and leave a mess behind.

Chapter 14
Ram

After bringing Baby Zah home, Khadijah turned into a natural when it came to mothering. She kept a chart for her breastfeeding schedule and a record of soiled diapers so she could accurately report it to Zahir's pediatrician. Outside of a few doctor's appointments, she didn't leave home for two weeks. Khadijah did have business to tie up at her school for her upcoming graduation ceremony. She needed to make sure she didn't owe any money on books and sign off on her cap and gown. She gave a few friends a heads up that she would be there so they could see the baby. She dressed Zahir so cute, making sure his hat and booties matched his little red and black outfit.

As Khadijah sat in the front office of the school waiting to see her counselor, Zahir got hungry. Khadijah had only been surrounded by people in support of breastfeeding so she didn't think twice about throwing a modesty blanket over her shoulder and nursing him.

A few girls that she knew walked over.

"Aww, you had the baby. Lemme see!" One snatched off the modesty blanket. She jumped back and immediately felt bad for exposing Khadijah's breast. "My bad...wait? You do that? Do it hurt?"

Khadijah smiled while covering herself back up. "It's okay, girl. Yes, it's uncomfortable at first but its best for my baby's immunity and growth. It's also cheaper."

The girl laughed."I know that's right. 'Cause milk is too high! Congratulations though, he is too cute!"

Khadijah smiled and felt so grown. She knew a lot for her age. As she finished nursing her baby and started to burp him, in walked that dang on Probability and Statistics teacher.

"Hey, Khadijah Mason!" she said with a fake smile. "Congratulations on your new bundle of joy. Mrs. Klein told me how you did your final from the hospital bed. You didn't have to, I would've understood."

"No, you were clear about me having to complete it to graduate so I did what I had to do. But thanks for a good grade and nice year," Khadijah replied, annoyed. Zahir let out a loud burp, almost as if he cosigned for his mother. It was so sweet and predicting of the relationship they would soon have.

Zahir was Khadijah's road dog for everything. When graduation came he was only 4 weeks old, but he was there grinning for his mama. When fall came and Khadijah was tired from college schoolwork, Zahir was there bouncing happily to keep her spirits up. When Jose continued to break promises as well as her heart, Zahir was there.

After another year of Jose dogging Khadijah out by lying, breaking promises, and even infecting her with a curable STD, she was finally ready to get off the Jose train. One-year-old Zahir was right there, loving his mama and being her consistent light.

The next five years of Khadijah's life were beautiful, but she was definitely on cruise control. After she shed the dead weight of Jose, she started working as a makeup artist for a mineral makeup brand and did hair on the side. She was determined to get a car before her 20th birthday. Khadijah paid for cab rides and bus fare to get around and it was becoming a pain in the ass. So she set yearly goals.

She set a goal of getting a car by 20 and did it. After falling behind on a traditional path of school, she regrouped and made a decision to become a licensed esthetician. She was very optimistic about the growing field and wanted to go to school for something that would have a quick return on investment. She also set a goal to get a higher paying job. So within the next year, Khadijah got a better paying job in the field and became an esthetician. Her next few goals were more personal.

At 21, she was in her career, had a car she owned, had a very smart three-year-old, and had a social life people would kill for. However, on the inside she was a jumbled mess. Khadijah began drinking heavier, smoking cigarettes and weed occasionally. She also entertained multiple men. Khadijah was going through what most women affectionately call her "hoe phase." She hid it well but knew that her lifestyle choices would get the best of her.

Khadijah had a pregnancy scare and contracted another curable STD. Having no idea who the father would be or who infected her, she privately booked an appointment with a therapist. She had issues and needed to get them resolved. Black women, especially young black women, had a terrible opinion of therapy and related it with being crazy, so she didn't tell any of her friends. Khadijah also felt a little separated from God. He had done so much for her and her actions didn't equate to gratitude.

So her goal for that year was to get her mind and spirit on one accord. After multiple counseling sessions and a few drop in visits to a church she heard about from her friend's mother, she was meeting yet another goal. That 5-year period of Khadijah's life was a prerequisite for her own personal love story. She had a feeling in the back of her mind that whoever her future prince charming was would not approve of the direction her life was going in. The changes she was making to better herself were necessary.

Khadijah's mind was made up that a man other than Jose would be her future husband. Jose moved to a different state, had more kids, got sent to prison, and neither him nor his family regarded Zahir. Having experienced abandonment in the past, that was all it took for her to 100% over him.

Khadijah had been working on her finances, career, mind, spirit, and overall self. She was becoming a dream woman for some lucky man. She even took a pledge of celibacy to complete the transformation she was making for herself and her son.

By choice, Khadijah and Zahir still lived with her mom. Jen and Khadijah got along like roommates. It had been 2 years since her brother Hasaan moved out. He had a girlfriend and a baby of his own so it was always just Jen, Khadijah, and Zah. The peace she found was so beautiful. She even started to get picky with her friendships. She was on a divine purpose to puncture every curse that was projected for her and her future.

The summer before her 23rd birthday, an old friend named Marcus inboxed Khadijah's Facebook. Marcus went to high school with her at The Ville and played on the drumline when she was a Villesette. He claimed to have always had a crush on her.

Marcus was 6'2" and about 260 lbs. He was biracial so he had very light brown skin, perfect white teeth, and silky black hair. He wore hats a lot because his hair was beginning to recede, but he always dressed nicely and smelled good. Khadijah thought he was cute but she was not about to relinquish her newly found peace to a man that she didn't trust. Her usual type was a dark skinned man that was unapologetically black. Khadijah was incredibly Afrocentric and was turned off by toxic blackness. She associated Marcus' lighter skin to him being detached from the black experience. She was so judgmental. Marcus also had a four-year-old son. She wondered where the mother was. Khadijah had no time for baby mama drama. She was living her best life and couldn't afford a disturbance.

Marcus made it his business to ask Khadijah on dates religiously. He asked her on a date to a baseball game, a bbq, out for drinks, and he even asked her to be in one of his music videos. He had an amateur singing career and figured she would say yes to an opportunity like that. All women liked attention right?

Khadijah was a hard shell to crack. She turned down all of his offers one by one. As far as the music video, she told Marcus that she preferred to be behind the camera and would give him a discount for her makeup artistry services if he booked her.

Khadijah was annoyed, but intrigued by his consistency. She'd never had a man pursue her so fiercely. After she turned down the music video cameo, Khadijah decided to get advice from the wisest woman she knew, her mother.

Jen had evolved so much in her seven years of sobriety. She was a doting grandmother and a strong woman determined to return to a balanced life.

One day as Jen was cooking dinner, Khadijah approached her.

"Hey, Jennifer!" She said, jokingly.

"Girl, you know my name ain't Jennifer! I hate when people call me that and it's Mama to you!"

"I'm just kidding, Mama," Khadijah cleared up. "So there's this guy that I been friends with and he calls himself trying to like me. He's cool but too light skin...and he has a baby...but he keeps asking me out."

"Does he have a Facebook? Pull him up," Jen asked so she could use her investigative skills to lurk.

"Yes, he does. Here he is," Khadijah said as she handed her mom the phone.

"Look Mommy! I drew you a picture!" squealed Zahir, disturbing their nosey moment. He was very artistically inclined and loved his mama's attention. Deep inside, Zahir was another reason Khadijah avoided anything serious with anyone. Her baby deserved the best. She refused for anyone else to walk out on him. She kissed Zahir and complimented him on yet another work of art and sent him to play. She was eager to hear Jen's opinion.

After Jen lurked on Marcus' page, she was ready for a verdict.

"Khadijah, this is a nice, handsome, young man. His teeth are white, he loves his mama and takes care of his son. Its woman out here that'll accept less. Go on a date with that boy," she proclaimed in a serious tone as she stirred the food she was cooking. Khadijah giggled and walked off while responding to Marcus' last invitation to a dinner of her choice. She replied through her Facebook inbox.

"I'd love to join you for dinner. I love sushi and know a nice restaurant on the other side of town."

Marcus called Khadijah's phone as soon as she sent the message. This man was serious about showing interest. As wonderful of a trait as it was, Khadijah wasn't used to that. She was used to men being nonchalant and playing hard to get.

"Hello?" Khadijah answered, cooly.

"Hey pretty lady," Marcus said in his sexy voice. "I just want you to know I'm excited to take you out. I been had my eyes on you."

Bashful, Khadijah flirted back. "Well, now I got my eyes on you, too."

They both laughed and caught up. They'd talked on the phone in the past but just as friends. Marcus opened up a new side of Khadijah that he didn't know. He loved how mysterious and particular she was. He also loved how much she adored her son. It was refreshing for him. Marcus had full custody of Lil Marc ever since he was 5 months old. His mother was reckless and abusive. Observing Lil Marc's straight hair and pale skin led Khadijah to believe that his mother was probably a white woman. Marcus confirmed she was. It was a hard pill to swallow that she was content with not being in her son's life. None of her family was in his life either. Marcus's mom and his family were all that Lil Marc had.

Khadijah explained to Marcus how her and Jose drifted apart and he faded out of Zahir's life as well. He was finishing a prison sentence of 4 years. They assured each other that those chapters were closed.

They both had love to give and were eager to meet each other's children. Marcus was serious about making the best impression he could on Khadijah. Not only did he buy a new outfit but he sent her a picture of it for approval. It was the sweetest, corniest thing she'd ever witnessed. He was too good to be true.

Date night came and Khadijah wore a black silky blouse with a fitted knee length pencil skirt. She wore her red natural hair in a Mohawk with minimal jewelry and beat her face to the gawds. She finished off her look with all black, suede peep toe Steve Madden heels that tied around the ankle and a leather black clutch. She texted Marcus when she was about to valet so he could meet her outside. When he laid eyes on Khadijah, his mouth dropped. Her oiled up thick legs glistened in the night. She was a diamond and he knew it. He took her hand as she took a few small steps into the sushi restaurant.

They stared at each other, had small talk, and smiled until their cheeks hurt. Marcus told Khadijah over and over how beautiful she was. When it was time to order, Khadijah showed off and ordered without glancing at the menu. She started with edamame and then, by memory, ordered her favorite sushi rolls and favorite martini.

Marcus ordered a drink, a specialty burger and fries. She teased him for not ordering sushi. He joked that he had to act like he did to secure the date. They talked about dreams, each other's kids, headaches, past love, and what they wanted for the future. It was literally something out of a fairy tale. As their date came to an end, Marcus graciously paid the bill and tipped the waitress $50. Khadijah was impressed.

"Did you Valet?"

"No, baby I didn't."

Khadijah thought he was slick as oil, already sliding pet names into their conversation. "Oh, well do you want me to drive you to your car?"

"...No, I walked," he said, smiling. "My mom stays around the corner."

Khadijah felt bad for asking, but was impressed that he walked to their first date. She really wanted to help him. "Can I at least drop you off at her house?"

"It's fine, babe. I have to work an overnight shift. That's why I have my bag. My work clothes are already with me. I'll call you when I make it."

Khadijah's mouth dropped. Marcus walked to their first date and then had to work an overnight shift at his second job. She felt so special. She hugged him and smelled his cologne as they prepared to depart. His touch was so assuring. Khadijah was ready to abandon that celibacy pledge. They thanked each other for a wonderful and exciting date night, she got in her car, and drove off. Her mind was gone. She couldn't believe how wonderful that date was.

When Khadijah got home, her mom had Zahir tucked in and asleep. She put on her pjs and laid down, feeling like she was on cloud nine. Khadijah got on her Facebook to have something mindless to do as she settled down. She noticed Marcus changed his relationship status.

Khadijah had deep seeded trust issues, so she always thought the worst. She assumed he maybe got caught by his secret girlfriend and changed his relationship status to assure her that their date meant nothing. Shortly after she figured it out, Marcus called Khadijah's phone.

"Hello?" She answered with an attitude.

"Hey, Khadijah. I can't get you off of my mind....you know I-" he said, innocently.

"Look Marcus," Khadijah said, cutting him off. "Before you came along, I was minding my own business. I was doing me...just fine. Then here you come trying to sell me this love story. I saw you change your relationship status. If you had a girlfriend, you should've said so. Don't play with my heart or sell me no damn dreams!" she snapped.

"Khadijah, I changed my status because I wanted to date you exclusively. I want to be in a relationship with you. I can send you a relationship request if you don't believe me," he said with a smile.

Khadijah felt so silly and childish. She wasn't used to good, intentional men. She had so many walls up, it was sad.

"Oh...I'm sorry...umm yeah, go ahead and send it," she said, calling his bluff.

Marcus Haven listed you as 'In a Relationship' Accept or Decline.

Khadijah accepted it. Just like that, they were boyfriend and girlfriend.

Chapter 15
Worthy or Not

No tarot reading or prophecy could prepare Khadijah for how fast her relationship with Marcus would grow. Within two months of dating, he was professing his love. Even though Khadijah was afraid to, she loved him back. Marcus was determined to date with purpose. He wanted to court Khadijah. They went on real dates and dressed up for one another. Sadly, her celibacy pledge ended, but he was one hell of a lover. Luckily, she was on a reliable birth control. Marcus was a Scorpio and he made love to Khadijah with all of his heart, mind, and body. With him, Khadijah felt like they were having an exchange of love instead of her feeling like she was giving herself away. Frequently, she would shed a tear of joy at climax. She didn't know that she could feel that good. She didn't know her body had a natural high locked inside. Marcus had the key. He showed her everyday that she was his prize, but Khadijah felt like the lucky one.

They arranged play dates with the children. If they were serious, they understood that each other's child was an extension of them. Zahir was 5 and Lil Marc was 4 so when they did meet, they clicked up like old pals. Zahir liked "Big Marcus and Lil Marc" as he affectionately called them. Lil Marc started asking to spend more time with Khadijah as well.

It meant so much to Marcus that Khadijah spent time with Lil Marc. All he ever wanted was a wife and mother for his son. Khadijah wanted the same. They were each other's missing puzzle pieces.

After six months of actively dating, they decided to move in together. It was definitely too soon in their extended family's opinion. They had been going to church together more and more. Some people accused them of trying to shack up. Marcus and Khadijah felt that pooling their finances together would provide more stability for their children. They both agreed that the goal was to be engaged within a year of moving in together. It was against their religion to shack up, but hopefully God would bless their good intentions.

Jen was really happy for her daughter, but she also knew that Khadijah had a lot to learn about financial responsibility. However, Khadijah wasn't a child anymore so Jen respected her wishes. She just assured Khadijah that if she moved out, it would be because of her own choice. Jen would never put her out.

Marcus' extended family was a different story. Though well intended, his family was very judgmental and cautious. In their opinion, they didn't know Khadijah like that. His mother was also very cautious as well. They ultimately didn't want to see the relationship fail and watch Lil Marc go through instability.

However, Khadijah had a hard time seeing things from his family's perspective and assumed that they just didn't care for her. Regardless of opinions, the move happened.

It was an interesting transition. Marcus and Khadijah found a very nice 2 bedroom apartment across the street from a nice, big park. They had a housewarming for their cute, new apartment. While Khadijah was still confused on how her potential in-laws would treat her, she was grateful for the way they showered them with love and support. They all came to the house warming with nice gifts to help them settle in and they even washed dishes and cleaned before they left. They may not have been the type of family to be sentimental with words, but their actions were helpful and for that Khadijah was grateful.

"Blended family woes" became a frequent Google search for Khadijah in the upcoming months. Marcus had a way of doing things and so did she. They bumped heads with everything under the sun. What they ate for dinner. How Lil Marc didn't like vegetables. How Zahir drank Sprite. How much responsibility and chores the boys needed for their age. Bedtime. What brand of medicine the children would take for illnesses.

One issue that really bothered Khadijah was the way Marcus' mother hovered over Lil Marc. She unconsciously prevented Khadijah and Lil Marc from building their own bond. Marcus' mother also showed little interest in building a relationship with Zahir. Khadijah was persistent in trying to win Lil Marc over, but children feel the boundaries that adults set. It was definitely an uphill battle.

Meanwhile, Marcus and Zahir were two peas in a pod. They horse played together. Marcus cuddled Zahir as if he was his son by blood and grew very protective of him. Khadijah was a little jealous that they hit it off so easily. She had a heart to love Lil Marc like her own but she wasn't given the full opportunity to be a mother figure. She thought that perhaps time would heal this thorn in her foot.

Khadijah and Marcus were so in love and dedicated to one another, that all of those issues brought them closer together. Money flowed from both of their incomes and they had big plans for one another.

As promised, On November 11th, 2013, Marcus proposed to Khadijah at home. She said yes! She picked out her own ring and was very excited to plan their forever. All Khadijah had been to a man up until this point was a baby mama and a girlfriend. She daydreamed about becoming Marcus' wife.

It seemed as soon as they were engaged, all hell broke loose. Khadijah began having a terribly strained relationship with her brother.

Over the years, Hasaan became a loner, to say the least. Khadijah accepted her brother for who he was but often felt as if their relationship was based on survival and not love. Khadijah knew that the trauma the two of them faced in their childhood had taken a toll on him. She yearned for a meaningful relationship with her brother that included quality time and an actually being apart of each other's lives.

Hasaan had a lot of secrets and was sometimes explosive with Khadijah when she tried to know more about his life. After many failed attempts of forging a healthy sibling relationship, she gave up. Khadijah needed to focus on her new future with Marcus.

Many of her friends started to show their true colors as well. Over the years, Khadijah had been the type to go the extra mile for her friends. While they dated and lived frivolously, she cheered them on and supported them selflessly. However, now that it was her time to shine, they were all ghost. If they were around, they had strong opinions against Marcus. They felt he didn't have enough money or clout.

Khadijah opened up to one of her close friends, Cici, about how she saw a future with Marcus. Cici was a single bachelorette who didn't have any children and viewed man eating as a sport. Cici accused khadijah of settling.

"I'm sorry Khadijah, he don't have enough money, baby. Being happy aint always enough," Cici preached.

Khadijah shut her down quickly. "The little he does have, he gives it all to me. He loves me and goes out of his way to show it."

Cici knew Khadijah yearned to be loved and deep down inside she knew Marcus was a good catch. A part of her wished she bagged him before Khadijah.

Many of her friends came up with bogus reasons to oppose her relationship. They also didn't like that Marcus empowered Khadijah to say no to them sometimes.

One friend even demanded Khadijah do her makeup for Khadijah's own wedding day. Khadijah knew it was her fault. Over the years, her people pleasing got so bad that everyone around her never heard her say no. They were used to Khadijah being at their disposal. How dare she do something for herself?

Marcus lost his main job three months into the engagement. He felt so helpless. They had already paid deposits on the major components of the wedding; the church, reception venue, photographer, and Khadijah's dress. They were in too deep to walk away. He was the man of the house and had to rely on Khadijah to help with their bills and obligations. Although it really hurt his manhood, he got a chance to see Khadijah wear her ride or die cape. This was real life and if they could withstand these trials, then they could jump the broom confidently.

They continued to go to church, tithe, and go to their couple's counseling sessions. With the help of their loved ones, returned favors, and kept promises, they made it to their wedding day.

On September 6th, 2014, the two became one.

The wedding was a dream come true. Marcus and Khadijah were blessed by live singers, a live band, and songs that pulled heartstrings tighter than a violin. What was meant to be, was and who was meant to be there, was there.

Marcus had his beard shaped up perfectly. He wore a grey tailored suit with champagne gold accents. Zahir and Lil Marc matched him, minus the beard. Khadijah wore a soft white ball gown with a flower sash. Her hair was in a classic bun with sparkling accessories. Her makeup was soft and fresh.When Marcus laid eyes on his bride as she walked down the aisle, he cried like a baby.

They were surrounded by love and family but what mattered most was that they had each other. Marcus kept his promise. He made a wife out of Khadijah. She looked beyond his faults to loved and respect him for who he was.

Joined together, they were now Marcus and Khadijah Haven. After the wedding, Khadijah realized she had checked so much off of her goals checklist that she made for herself.

Was she worthy or not? The answer was yes.

Chapter 16
For Real, For Real

Even though finances were tight, Khadijah and Marcus were living life to the fullest. Marcus was an affectionate man so he often romanced Khadijah with creative date nights. The two of them would coordinate their outfits and make sure they looked and smelled rich. People would stop them in public just to tell them how beautiful of a couple they were.

Jen was very supportive during this time in their lives. She was always one call away. A few years prior, she told Khadijah to be careful with the birth controls she experimented with. Jen wanted her daughter to live a long, healthy life. Taking her mother's advice, Khadijah agreed to lay off of the birth control just in case her and Marcus ever decided to have one more child.

Khadijah had such negative experiences with past pregnancies that she didn't really know if she wanted to go down that road again. Lil Marc may not have been of her blood, but he was her second son. Him and Zahir were more than enough. Children were expensive. Priceless, but expensive.

As her passion for the makeup artistry grew, Khadijah started freelancing. She made business cards online and began to build her before and after portfolio. She figured if she could make money as an artist for major companies and spas that she could do it for herself.

She encouraged Marcus to start focusing on his God-given talents as well. He was a hard worker by nature. No one had ever cared to help him cultivate his gifts until he got with Khadijah. He was good with his hands, coordinated, had an impeccable memory, and a pure heart. Jobs would get the two of them through hardships but careers needed to be established soon. Marcus had one big problem that he had ignored for years. He dropped out of high school and never received his GED. It embarrassed him and held him back from better opportunities. He knew that he had to become serious about retaining his GED in order to succeed for his family.

A few months after their wedding, the Haven's celebrated their first Christmas as a married family. Their Christmas before was nice, but it wasn't as sentimental as this year's. Marcus and Khadijah worked hard to make sure their children had a decorated tree, lights, stockings, a gingerbread house, and wrapped gifts under the tree. Little did they know, the best gift would come right after the new year.

Khadijah's birthday was ten days after Christmas, so people close to her tended to avoid her birthday. They usually spent all of their money so they couldn't afford to celebrate with her. Khadijah let this frustration be known to Marcus as soon as the two of them started dating. Marcus always listened intently whenever Khadijah gave him a key to making her happy.

So to keep his wife happy, Marcus went out of his way to book Khadijah and him a staycation at a nice hotel for her birthday weekend. She was so excited to kick back, have a glass of wine, and just be free with her husband. Due to financial restraint, they couldn't do a traditional honeymoon. However, one thing about the two of them was their shared optimism. They made lemonade out of every situation they ran into.

The day after celebrating the new year, Khadijah started to get pack for the staycation. She was rummaging through her closet, trying to find a mate to one of her favorite boots.

After standing up too fast, Khadijah had a queasy feeling and assumed it was PMS. She checked her period tracker app and discovered her period was late. Surely she hadn't gotten pregnant that fast! Her period just returned a month ago after years and years of birth control. She went to pee and recognized the smell of vitamins; her own quirky pregnancy symptom.

Resisting the possible truth, she asked Marcus to pick up a pregnancy test from the store. This wasn't their first scare, but this time felt different. Khadijah looked at herself in the mirror. She had just cut her hair similar to the hairstyle she wore when she was pregnant with Zahir. Was that a coincidence?

As she stared at her reflection, a different woman appeared other than the little girl she once knew. In the past, Khadijah was an abandoned, molested, judged, immature, irresponsible, promiscuous, insecure, and depressed baby mama. Her new self shined from the inside out. She was set free, set apart, business minded, loved, sober, and a wonderful mother and loving wife. The curse of a broken family was rebuked a long time ago. The curse of abuse was not welcome in their dwelling. The curse of recklessness died with her choosing a better path. She was the spiritual reset button for her family.

Hearing Marcus' voice brought Khadijah out of her trance. She never heard him come in the front door. He had the pregnancy test ready. Khadijah ripped it open and followed the directions by peeing on the stick. Her and Marcus waited anxiously.

"Are you nervous?" Marcus asked Khadijah.

Khadijah bit her lips. "...Kind of."

One minute....

Two.

Three.

Four.

As soon as the fifth minute passed they looked at the test nervously. Two dark pink lines appeared on the pregnancy stick. Khadijah was indeed pregnant. She took a second test just to make sure and it was positive, too!

Khadijah began to cry and hyperventilate. All of her affirmations went out of the window and every fear whisked right back in. Every bad memory followed that fear. This love story was too good to be true. Marcus would leave her just like Jose did, just like her father did, and just like her other family and friends did.

Marcus interrupted her negative thoughts. "Khadijah, don't cry baby. Don't you want to have my baby?" He asked in the sweetest, most genuine tone. Khadijah embraced him so tight. "I love you and I got you and this baby," he assured her.

Khadijah wiped her eyes. "I know you love me, Marcus. I'm just so scared."

In Khadijah's experience, talk was cheap. She was all about actions. Positive actions were the only antidote for all of the negative experiences she had.

Khadijah's pregnancy started out with morning, midday, and night sickness. She could hardly keep any food down. She was embarrassed, but Marcus rubbed her back everytime she threw up. He made sure he picked up after the boys more because he knew how much tidiness made Khadijah happy. He told Khadijah how beautiful she was without makeup on days he knew she didn't have the strength to put any on. Marcus even cuddled her to sleep every single night so she could feel safe.

Marcus righted every single wrong from Khadijah's past during that entire pregnancy. He punctured another curse. He waited on Khadijah hand and foot and he went to every doctor's appointment happily by choice. He prayed for her and the baby nightly and interacted with the baby while counting kicks. He was the best husband and father anyone could ask for.

Khadijah still had acute morning sickness towards the end of her pregnancy. Not being able to work consistently caused them to fall behind on bills. They were three months away from a new baby and with two growing boys and revolving bills, they were falling into a deep pit.

One day when they were all sitting at home, they heard a loud knock at the door.

"It betta be the police," Khadijah muttered while folding clothes. Marcus went to answer the door and Khadijah heard a deep voice. It was a sheriff serving papers.

When Marcus walked back into the room, he stared at Khadijah and her round belly.

"What is it?" Khadijah asked.

Marcus' lip began to tremble. "We're getting evicted."

This was a familiar hurt for Khadijah, but the sting was fresh. Eviction was the initial news that lead to Jen's addiction years ago.

How could this happen?

The landlord couldn't afford for them to have anymore extensions so he filed for them to be evicted.

Khadijah quickly empathized with how her mother may have felt when she went through this same thing years ago. She called her mother to let her know what was happening. Jen offered loving advice. Advice couldn't pay bills.

While their children were at school, Khadijah and Marcus got on their knees and prayed daily for a way out. They also applied for different programs that offered affordable housing. They both felt so hopeless and irresponsible, but sulking wasn't an option for their innocent children that would be affected by doing nothing at all.

It was just revealed to them at a recent doctor's appointment that they were having a daughter so this sounded all too familiar for Khadijah. The curse must've been attached to her. Khadijah's anxiety had a field day with her mind. All of the beautiful rehabilitation her self-esteem and mind had undergone was in vain. This plague, this curse really wanted her. However, it had yet to encounter the power of God.

Within a week, Marcus got a call from an apartment complex that offered income-based rent. Marcus was surprised because he applied for that apartment long before him and Khadijah were even an item. He applied for him and Lil Marc when he found out he would be a single father. The apartments told him that he would be placed on a waiting list and he never heard from them again.

He asked the receptionist if his application was still viable considering the increase in the size of his family. He inherited a wife, an bonus son, and a baby on the way. They assured Marcus that as long as he had the financial need, the offer was still valid.

At first, the Haven's were hesitant to accept the apartment due to the bad neighborhood but they understood that it would be a stepping stone for their future. They had to weigh the pros and cons. Times like these required logical adulting, not emotional opinions.

The neighborhood was indeed considered the projects. The complex was always on the news for a shooting or crime. However, the projects had recently undergone renovations. They also switched to new management. After going back and forth, they decided to accept the apartment.

It was so hard to move from their dream apartment to the projects but there was a peace in knowing they had escaped homelessness. Khadijah felt guilty that she allowed pride to belittle what was actually a blessing.

After getting settled into their new apartment in the projects they realized that the neighborhood was rough, but not nearly as bad as the rumors led them to believe.

Marcus started to get nervous about how much time he had to better himself. He was hardworking and loved his family and wanted his efforts to match.

Marcus was offered a free GED class after workers from the leasing office learned he was a high school dropout. He was determined to be a good example to his children. He asked Khadijah to help him study for the test. He told her how he wasn't the best at taking tests. Good thing Khadijah was a natural teacher and nurturer. She strategized and came up with a foul proof study plan to help her husband pass his GED.

A pregnant Khadijah and a desperate Marcus spent hours watching Schoolhouse Rock videos to prepare him for his GED test. They were resilient about their children, present and unborn, having the best opportunities possible.

The day he had to go in for testing, Khadijah made Marcus a great big breakfast. She made buttermilk biscuits with gravy, sausage, bacon, fluffy cheese eggs, sugar rice, and a small cup of fruit. She also made him a savory cup of sweet coffee with hazelnut creamer.

They all ate breakfast together in a celebratory manner for the man of the house. They also prayed that testing anxiety or fear did not get in the way of him and his goal of passing.

Marcus passed his GED with flying colors.

This meant so much for him. He often shared with Khadijah that he never really felt like he was smart after dropping out of high school. He was so grateful and proud of himself. Things really were looking up for The Haven's.

A week after acing his GED, they received a letter that they had been anticipating. The letter read, "Congratulations, you've been accepted into the Welcome Home Program. Homeownership is in your near future. Please call us to book your first appointment."

Tears flowed from Marcus and Khadijah's eyes. The Welcome Home Project offered affordable mortgage rates and home insurance to qualified families. They used volunteer work and participation in wellness workshops as collateral for home buying incentives.

Life finally felt good. It felt safe.

Chapter 17

Here she Comes

Khadijah was so tired of being pregnant. She had passed her official due date and because of her discomfort they would induce her for delivery.

Because it was now planned, Khadijah was able to carefully pack and double check her hospital bag and make plans for the boys. Jen and Marcus' mothers both agreed to help with the boys.

The magical day came and it was reminiscent of a show Khadijah used to watch as a young girl called, "A Baby Story." Marcus massaged Khadijah and prayed for her and the baby as she labored.

When it was time to push, the room was so serene. Khadijah held her husband's hands tightly as if in an intense game of tug of war. She thankfully stared into his face. Only the doctor and one nurse were in the room with them. When she delivered Zah, Khadijah recalled being comforted by a room full of people.

However, this quiet room was just as comfortable. It was a physical and spiritual rebirth for Khadijah. She had pressed the reset button. As each contraction came, she pushed. Khadijah didn't scream and barely grunted. She was focused. This baby would be born into love. This baby would serve as a walking, talking reminder that the curses that plagued Khadijah had to bow to the grace and mercy of God.

After the final push, Khadijah felt a release that made her feel weightless. Khalia Amirah Haven, their "together baby," came into the world on September 10, 2015 at 8:20am. She was healthy, cuddly, and beautiful. She was the glue that made this blended family, a true family. It was love at first sight when the boys got to meet their baby sister.

Khadijah was different this time around. Her joy had no boundaries. Seeing her sons bond and have a healthy relationship with Khalia gave her strength. Knowing Khalia had a father that adored her and was just as invested in protecting her as she was, gave her life. The fatherless curse was finally dismantled. She would walk in the spirit of grace and prosperity moving forward. Everything would be alright. It had to.

Khadijah rocked her new baby girl with a new mindset, determined to be the best her that she could be. Full of life. A dreamer. A conquerer. A wife. A mother of 3.

Remembering the song her mother used to sing, Khadijah hummed while rocking her newborn baby.

"That's why darling it's incredible...that someone so unforgettable...thinks that I am...unforgettable, too."

Exclusive Sneak Peek

Puncturing the Deepest Curse Part 2

"Khadijah couldn't believe her eyes. Her stomach was in shambles. Her hopes and dreams were crushed. Her heart was broken into a million pieces.

Khadijah's eyes began to flow with tears so strong she could've drowned. Her brain was moving a million times faster than normal. How could this type of invasion come into her life? How could it come for her marriage?

Khadijah was a wonderful wife. Sure, she gained some extra weight but it was in the right places. Khadijah cooked the most flavorful, delicious meals. She cleaned up after her family as if she'd receive a badge of honor. She kept herself up, contributed to the household financially, adored her children, went to church, loved on her in-laws and kept it tight in the bedroom. Even at that moment her lips were dry and numb and her hips were sore as hell from pleasing her husband the night before.

It appeared Marcus was happy overall. Lately, he was a little unhappy with himself but that wouldn't lead him to unfaithfulness, would it?

These screenshots had her husband's name attached to them but this man's tone and words were not Marcus'.

The dates on these messages fell on common, family-time hours. If this was indeed Marcus texting this woman, he did it right under Khadijah's nose.

Marcus was a man of great character. He was God-fearing and spoke strongly against extramarital affairs. This had to be a mix up. This woman had no reason to lie.

Zahir, Lil Marc, and Khalia peeked their heads around the corner from their room. Zahir and Lil Marc were old enough to know that they should stay in their room because grown folks were talking. Khalia was a toddler so she didn't know any better. She slowly walked over to Khadijah and the visitor sitting on the couch and rubbed her mother's face.

Khadijah scooped up Khalia, searching for comfort. Khalia wiped her mother's crying eyes. "Don't cry, Mommy."

Khadijah had to cry. She wanted to break but her children were the glue that kept her from losing it. Crying was her only option.

Khadijah looked at her surroundings. They still lived in the projects. It was hard enough to be encouraged when things were peachy. Now she had to encourage herself in a low place she thought she'd never be. She had been working like a slave and would come home to such a depressing neighborhood. The tiny apartment closed in on her as she took each breath. Her sadness morphed into anger.

"How the hell can he even afford to cheat?"

Khadijah was consumed by bitterness, betrayal, anger, vengefulness, and confusion. She stared into Khalia's face. Her caramel complexion, honest eyes, and chunky cheeks were so precious. Staring at her youngest child was bittersweet. Khalia had Marcus' face.

Made in the USA
Monee, IL
16 July 2020